D1624979

ALSO BY RICHARD PAUL EVANS

The Gift
Finding Noel
The Sunflower
A Perfect Day
The Last Promise
The Christmas Box Miracle
The Carousel
The Looking Glass
The Locket
The Letter
Timepiece
The Christmas Box

For Children
The Dance
The Christmas Candle
The Spyglass
The Tower
The Light of Christmas

✳RICHARD PAUL EVANS✳

Grace

**Doubleday Large Print
Home Library Edition**

SIMON & SCHUSTER

NEW YORK   LONDON   TORONTO   SYDNEY

Manufactured in the United States of America

ISBN-13: 978-1-60751-088-8

✶ ACKNOWLEDGMENTS ✶

The writing of Grace has been a remarkable journey. I would like to thank my fellow sojourners. First, my friends at Simon & Schuster: Carolyn Reidy, David Rosenthal, Sydny Miner, and Gypsy da Silva.

Also, my agent, Laurie Liss. (Unbelievably, I still love you after all these years.)

My writing assistant, Karen Berg-Roylance. Thank you for your unending enthusiasm and inspiration. My friends, Jean Nielsen and Barbara Thompson—thank you for sparking the idea.

Thank you to my staff: Miche "Captain" Barbosa (Lee), Heather McVey (James),

Karen Christopherson (Al), Chrystal Hodges (Collin), Barry Evans (Brenda), and Meagen Bunten (James).

Thank you to the Christmas Box International staff: Lisa McDonald, Sherri Engar, Patty Rose, Elisabeth Williams, Jean Krisle, Doug Smith, and Jenna Evans Welch. Also, Rick Larsen, Dennis Webb, Bob Gay, and our friends at Operation Kids for assisting us with the Christmas Box Initiative.

As always, thank you to my family: Keri Lyn, Jenna & David, Allyson, Abi, McKenna, Michael, and Bello. I am proud of you all and grateful for your support. You are my home, my heart, and my reason for living.

Most of all, thank you to my loyal, dear readers who share my stories. Without you, none of this happens. Have a blessed Holiday season.

To Barry

✦ AUTHOR'S NOTE ✦

In the summer of 1874, Mary Ellen Wilson, a nine-year-old girl from New York City, was the most talked about child in America. The event that created a national media frenzy back then wouldn't make the back page of a rural newspaper today: Mary Ellen was abused by her parents.

The abuse was so severe that Mary Ellen likely would have died if she hadn't been rescued by Etta Wheeler, a Methodist missionary working in the girl's neighborhood.

Ms. Wheeler's initial efforts to help the child were fruitless. No one wanted to believe that child abuse existed, or even that it *could* exist. Because of this, there were no laws on the books prohibiting cruelty to children.

There were, however, laws prohibiting cruelty to animals. After repeated failures in her efforts to seek justice for Mary Ellen, the determined Wheeler took her case to Henry Bergh, the founder of the ASPCA, the American Society for the Prevention of Cruelty to Animals. Bergh and his organization won protection for Mary Ellen by arguing that a child was, in fact, a member of the animal kingdom, worthy of the same protection under law as a dog.

Despite national outrage over the case, the commotion quickly died down and people once again closed their eyes to the problem.

Shortly after the turn of the century, public recognition of child abuse faced another setback when renowned psychologist Sigmund Freud publicly theorized that his patients' claims of childhood sexual abuse were merely repressed fantasies.

It wasn't until the early 1960s, nearly a century after the Wilson case, that the medical profession formally agreed upon the existence of child abuse.

While the world debated whether or not child abuse existed, thousands of children carried horrible secrets and scars, both physical and emotional; because no one would believe or protect them. Many of them ran away from home.

Grace is the story of one of those children.

"It were better for him that a millstone were hanged about his neck, and he cast into the sea, than that he should offend one of these little ones."

✦ LUKE 17:2 ✦

Grace

✴ THE LITTLE MATCH GIRL ✴
By Hans Christian Andersen

It was Christmas Eve, and from the brightly lit windows of the town square came the sound of laughter and singing as people celebrated the holiday. Outside, the snow-covered streets were deserted except for the poor little match seller who sat alone beside a frozen fountain. Her ragged dress and worn shawl did little to protect her from the cold. She hadn't sold one box of matches all day and she was frightened to go home, for her father would certainly punish her. She was so cold. If only she could light a match, she thought, but she knew her father would beat her for wasting.

She resisted until it was too cold to bear any longer. She took out a match and lit it. She magically saw in its light a large stone hearth with a brilliant fire. Beyond the hearth was a fine table laden with food. As she reached out towards the table, the match went out and the magic faded. Her eyes filled with tears.

She struck another match and an even more wonderful vision appeared. Before her was a Christmas tree hung with hundreds of candles, glittering with tinsel and colored balls.

"Oh, how lovely!" she exclaimed. Then, the flame flickered out. The light from the Christmas candles rose higher and higher. Then one of the lights fell, leaving a trail behind it. "Someone is dying," said the little girl, remembering what her beloved Grandmother used to say: "When a star falls, a heart stops beating!"

The little match seller lit another match. This time, she saw her grandmother.

"Grandma, stay with me! I'm cold and alone!" She lit one match after the other, so that her grandmother would not disappear like all the other visions. When she was down to her last match, she cried out, "Grandma, take me away with you!" Her Grandmother smiled and opened her arms to the girl.

Christmas morning dawned, and a pale sun shone down on the frozen town square. On the snowy ground near the base of a fountain lay the lifeless body of a little girl surrounded by spent matches.

"Poor little thing," said a passerby. "She was trying to keep warm."

But by that time, the little match girl was far away where there is no cold, hunger nor pain.

CHAPTER

One

My memory of her has grown on my soul like ivy climbing a home until it begins to tear and tug at the very brick and mortar itself.

✴ ERIC WELCH'S DIARY ✴

DECEMBER 25, 2006

It's Christmas day. There is Christmas music playing from the radio in the other room. Mitch Miller's "Santa Claus Is Coming to Town." It's a little late, I think; Santa's come and gone, as have our children and grandchildren. They've left an impressive mess in their wake, but I don't care. As I get older I've come to treasure any evidence of family. Snow is falling outside and all is peaceful and still. In such moments it is possible to believe that the world could still be good.

Something profound happened to me today. It started innocently enough—as most life-changing experiences do—with a request from my grandchildren to read them a Christmas story, "The Little Match Girl." I've never been a fan of the tale, but, like most grandparents, I'm not one to deny my grandchildren. As I read to them, something happened to me; by the end of the story I was crying. Four-year-old Ebony Brooke tried to console me. "It's okay, Grandpa," she said. "It's just a story."

It's not just a story, there really was a little match girl and she changed my life in ways I'm still trying to understand. Even the grandchildren sitting before me wouldn't be here if it wasn't for her. As important as she is to me, I've never shared her story. It's finally time that I did.

My memory, like my eyesight, has waned with age and I pray I can get the story right. Still, there are things that become clearer to me as I grow older. This much I know: too many things were kept secret in those days. Things that never should have been hidden. And things that should have.

Who was she? She was my first love. My first kiss. She was a little match girl who could see the future in the flame of a candle. She was a runaway who taught me more about life than anyone has before or since. And when she was gone my innocence left with her.

There is pain in bringing out these memories. I suppose I don't really know why I feel compelled to write at this time, only that I am. Maybe I want those closest to me to finally know what has driven me for all these years. Why, every Christmas, I occasionally slip away into my thoughts to someplace else. Or maybe it's just that I still love her and wonder, after all this time, if I can still find grace.

CHAPTER

Two

To choose the path is to choose the destination. But sometimes it seems that the path is under our feet even before we know we're walking.

✦ GRACE'S DIARY ✦

My story began in October of 1962 about ten days before the world was supposed to end. I think the Cuban Missile Crisis brought us as close as we've ever come as a species to extinction.

Even without the imminent threat of global destruction, the holidays looked pretty grim for my family. In November of that year my mom told us it would be a "Dickens Christmas," and she didn't mean the festive kind with merry carolers wassailing in nineteenth-century attire. She meant the real Dickensian landscape of debtor prisons and want.

My family—me, my parents, and my ten-year-old brother, Joel—had just moved from a palm-tree-lined suburb of Los Angeles to a blighted neighborhood in south Salt Lake City, just a few blocks from State Street with its nightclubs, bars, and pawnshops. My father, a construction worker, had contracted Guillain-Barré syndrome, a serious disorder in which the body's immune system attacks parts of the nervous system. It started with weakness in his legs and for several months he was paralyzed from the neck down; the doctors said that if it got any worse he'd have to be put on a respirator to breathe. Fortunately, it never progressed that far. The good news, they said, was that he would likely make a full recovery, at least physically. Our financial situation was a different matter.

The first big thing to go was our car, a '61 Chevrolet Impala convertible, which was a pretty fine car even by today's standards. What I remember most about it was the smell of the red vinyl seats on hot days. It also had electric locks, which Joel and I flipped up and down until Mom yelled at us to stop. Dad sold the Impala, purchasing in its stead an ugly used utility van from the phone company, which cost him just two hundred dollars. The van was yellow with wide brown stripes running across its sides. Joel dubbed it "The Bee," which was appropriate for more than its paint job. The van's motor made a high-pitched humming noise and it wobbled at high speeds, especially with Mom at the wheel.

The back seats had all been removed and there were no side windows. One whole wall was covered with metal shelves, cubbies, and drawers for holding tools and electrical supplies.

Things got worse. To Joel's, and my horror, our parents decided to move. My grandmother from Salt Lake City had passed away three years earlier leaving her home vacant. My mother and her seven siblings had inherited the house and couldn't agree on what to do with it. It was decided that we could live there until they came to a consensus, which, at the rate things were going, was a little less likely than a nuclear holocaust.

On the day we moved, Joel and I helped Mom load up the Bee. A few neighbors came over with going-away brownies and lemonade, and ended up staying to help as well. Dad just shouted orders from his bed. It drove us crazy but Mom said it made *him* crazy to be so helpless. I guess shouting at us made him feel useful. Fortunately we didn't have much left to pack.

The Bee pulled out of our driveway, with furniture and luggage tied to the roof. My mother drove the whole way, the passenger seat next to her piled high with boxes. My father sat on a La-Z-Boy in the back of the van, while Joel and I sat on and between boxes and bags, rearranging them as best we could for comfort.

The trip seemed to take forever as we abused our parents with the obligatory "How much longer?" and "Are we there yet?" Had we known our destination, we might not have complained so much about the journey.

Our new home was a warped, rat-infested structure that smelled like mold and looked like it might have fallen over in a strong wind—if it weren't for all the cracks in the walls that let the wind pass through. What was left of the paint on the exterior was peeling. The interior rooms were covered with wallpaper, most of it water-damaged with long rusted streaks running down the walls. Still, for a couple of boys from the California suburbs, the arrangement wasn't all bad. The house sat on nearly five wooded acres bordered on two sides by a creek that ran high enough to float an inner tube during the summer.

That summer we scaled every tree—and there were lots of them—worthy of climbing. We also valued the trees for the food they produced. Money was so tight that my mother had stopped buying luxuries like potato chips and ice cream and now brought home only staples: bread, peanut butter, flour, and an occasional chuck roast for Sunday dinner. The trees, however, generously bent with ripe fruit. There were Bartlett pear, crabapple, apricot, peach, plum, Bing cherry, red Delicious apple, even a black walnut. Every day that summer we ate fruit until we were full, which satisfied us, but more times than not gave us the runs.

Joel and I spent that summer alone together. Joel loved baseball so we played a lot of catch, though it bothered me that he was four years younger than me and had a better fast ball. We also engaged in a fair amount of insect torture. On the east side of our home, on the slope of the underground fruit cellar, we found a hill of ant lion pits. We'd capture ants and drop them into the pits, watching for the buried ant lion to suddenly emerge. If we felt more adventurous, we'd hunt grasshoppers in the tall grass of the back fields, incarcerating them in a glass jar. We'd try them for some indiscretion—like reckless hopping or ugliness—and summarily execute them, usually death by rock or BB gun firing squad. Every day was something new.

I don't remember whose idea it was to build the clubhouse. Years later Joel claimed it was his. Whoever's it was, we never could have anticipated the chain of events it set in place.

We had all the materials we needed to build. My grandfather, who died long before I was born, was a pharmacist by trade. He was also a builder, and sheets of weathered plywood were stacked up against the old greenhouse and warped two-by-fours were piled in the smelly, straw-floored cinder block chicken coop my grandfather had built fifty years earlier.

As far as clubhouses go, ours was pretty big, ten foot by twelve foot, half the size of our bedroom. It had a particleboard floor on which we nailed carpet. The ceiling was about six feet high, though it sagged quite a bit in the middle. We clearly lacked our father's and grandfather's building skills.

One afternoon Joel and I were taking a lunch break, eating tuna and pickle sandwiches on slices of wheat bread, when Joel said, "It's going to cave in when it snows."

"Probably," I said, with my mouth still full.

I studied the sagging ceiling until I saw a solution. After lunch we dragged a four-by-four beam from the chicken coop, cut six inches off the top with a rusted handsaw, then raised it in the middle of the room to brace the ceiling, pounding it fully upright with a sledgehammer. The pillar was useful in other ways. We put nails in it and used it to hang our flashlight and the transistor radio I got on my last birthday.

The fact that the ceiling was low was not a bad thing. We didn't plan to do much standing around and it was a certain deterrent to adults, though probably not as much as the size of the entry itself. The clubhouse's front (and only) door was only three feet high, which made it necessary to crawl into the clubhouse. Joel pointed out that this would be good in case of an attack, as it would make it easier to defend ourselves. I asked him who he thought might be attacking us. He thought about it a moment, then replied, "Well, you never know."

We did our best to furnish the place with the creature comforts of home. For entertainment we had chess, Chinese checkers, and Monopoly. We hung artwork: a framed paint-by-numbers landscape, a poster of Superman, and a poster my mother never would have approved of—a Vargas pinup. Earlier that year I had started to take an interest in girls (alien as they were to my actual experience), and while we were first exploring the garage, Joel came across the rolled-up Vargas. The poster was pretty tame by today's standards—a young woman posing in a bright red swimsuit—but for its time it was considered pretty risqué. For us it was definitely taboo. I assumed it was my grandfather's, which was all the more reason for my mother to never find out we had it.

Our carpet and most of our furnishings came from the garage, an A-frame structure with a steeply pitched tar roof and two large wooden doors that opened like a barn. My parents stored some of our belongings in the garage when we first arrived, but with the exception of a brief and unsuccessful hunt for some missing pots and pans, I don't think my mother ever set foot in the place. Probably because it was dark, smelly, and housed more rats than a research laboratory.

To Joel and me the garage was a wonderland that housed a million things to ignite a boy's imagination. There were large spring traps, tin washtubs, boxes of ancient *National Geographics*, a World War II GI helmet, and even a kerosene lantern with several containers of kerosene. Whenever we needed something we'd head to the garage where we'd either find what we were looking for or forget about it in the excitement of a greater discovery. Once we went in looking for a lamp and found a hand-pump brass fire extinguisher and an electric generator from an old telephone that produced enough voltage to knock you on your keister if you touched the contacts while someone wound the crank. To make our chess games more interesting, we attached wires to the generator—which the loser had to hold for one full crank. To this day Joel doesn't play chess.

On one of our expeditions we found a mattress in the rafters above the garage and pushed it down. It looked like generations of mice had made the mattress their home, but they all fled at our arrival (or died in the fall). We broomed off the mice droppings and a few dead mice, then dragged it to the clubhouse.

There was a water spigot inside our clubhouse, one of the old orange hand-lever types. We discovered it after we started building. Since we couldn't move it, we just built around it, later deciding it technically gave our clubhouse indoor plumbing.

Even better than plumbing was electricity. Joel found a light socket and an old yellow extension cord, which we ran from the garage. We hung it from the ceiling and attached a light bulb. That night we brought in our sleeping bags and slept there. We stayed up playing Go Fish and Rook while eating walnuts from our trees until two in the morning. When we finally turned out the light it was darker than a cave, which kind of scared Joel. The next time we slept out we plugged in a nightlight. It lit the clubhouse in an eerie UFO alien green, which was still better than total darkness.

One day I was sitting at the kitchen table drawing cartoons when Joel came running inside. "Hey, come out to the clubhouse," he said excitedly.

"What?"

"You gotta come see."

I followed him out and crawled through the door to be greeted by the astringent odor of fresh paint.

"What did you do?" I asked.

"I painted."

"It's purple."

"Yeah."

"It's *purple.*"

Joel frowned, angry that I hadn't appreciated his surprise and hours of work. "It's all there was."

"It looks . . . femmy."

Joel turned red. "It's all there was."

CHAPTER

Three

There's a new rock and roll band called The Beatles. I like their music. I think they might do well.

✦ GRACE'S DIARY ✦

That summer I worried a lot. I worried that we'd live in that crummy neighborhood forever, and I worried *a lot* about the approaching school year. I had heard stories about inner-city schools and I lived in terror of what it would be like to go to one.

I also worried about money, or our lack of it. Every now and then Joel and I would try to earn some, combing the neighborhood looking for work. We'd mow lawns and do other odd jobs, but it was a poor neighborhood so we never got paid much. Once we helped Mrs. Poulsen, a two-hundred-year-old lady who lived at the end of our street, clean out her garage. That place hadn't been touched for decades, evidenced by the yellowed GERMAN STORM TROOPERS INVADE POLAND headline on a newspaper we threw out. It took an entire day, leaving us dirty and exhausted. When we'd completed the job she gave us each fifty cents. I stopped Joel from throwing his quarters at her door after she shut it.

In spite of the wasted day, two good things came from that project. First, we acquired an old fruit dryer. It was a square plywood box with window-screen trays that slid inside, which Mrs. Poulsen had us carry out to the curb for garbage pickup. We dragged the dryer home on the back of our wagon and put it in our clubhouse. It actually worked and we began drying apricots into fruit leather, which, to us, tasted as good as any store-bought candy.

Second, we spent our day's earnings on milkshakes, which led to my job at McBurger Queen.

McBurger Queen was on State Street about six blocks from our home. The name of the restaurant was my boss's genius. My boss, Mr. Dick (that's not meant to be derogatory, it was his actual surname), believed that by combining the names of the most successful burger joints in America he would capitalize on thousands of dollars of free advertising and make himself rich. The Queen, as we employees called it, was one of those places that had more items on the menu than a Chinese restaurant. It had sixty different kinds of malts, from grasshopper to caramel cashew (my personal favorite) and almost as many food choices, from fish burgers to soft tacos. My boss also sold water softeners and Amway products, and we were required to keep a stack of brochures for both on the front counter near the cash register.

Mr. Dick trusted no one. He believed John F. Kennedy, Martin Luther King, and the Pope belonged to a secret organization conspiring to rule the world. He also believed that all his employees were thieves bent on eating his inventory, which was sometimes true but not as true as Mr. Dick believed. Once one of my coworkers saw him in the parking lot across the street spying on us through binoculars. The very week I started working at the place, Mr. Dick hauled three of his workers off to take polygraph tests. I don't know if that was legal or not, but in those days kids our age pretty much went along with everything adults said.

I knew about the tests because Gary, the assistant manager (a forty-year-old guy with chronic, maybe terminal, dandruff), showed me the actual test results from the lie detector machine with its accompanying graph. The interrogator asked questions like: Have you ever stolen money from the till? (No spike on the report.) Have you given away free food? (Small spike.) Do you eat French fries without paying for them? (The spike went off the chart.)

After the inquiry, one of my co-workers never returned; I still imagine him languishing in a gulag somewhere. Of course the shakedown was meant as intimidation for the rest of us and it worked reasonably well. So, for the most part, we rarely ate on the job, even the mistakes, like when someone ordered a hamburger with no ketchup and we put ketchup on it anyway. At least not without looking over our shoulder a few times before wolfing it down.

What made Mr. Dick's actions more

CHAPTER

Four

Junior High School is the armpit of life.

✷ GRACE'S DIARY ✷

It's been said that parents should give their children roots and wings. That was a perfect description of my parents. Even in a wheelchair, my father was a dreamer with his head in the clouds and my mother was the roots with both feet planted firmly on terra quaking firma. My mother was always afraid. Afraid we didn't have enough money, afraid her health would give out, afraid something might happen to one of us. Pretty much afraid of life. When my father got sick I think it was for her vindication that the gods really were out to get us.

Shortly after our arrival in Utah, my

mother got a day job working as a cashier at Warshaw's Food and Drug. Her job didn't pay much, but she brought home damaged canned goods and day-olds from the bakery, which helped with the grocery bills. For years I thought that all soup cans came with dents in them.

For most of her life my mother had struggled with depression, and our situation didn't help much. People didn't talk as much about depression in those days; in some religions it was still regarded as a sin. Science made people less sinful with the wonder drug Librium.

My mother worked all day, then came home at night, physically and emotionally spent. My father just kind of moped around the house, dreaming up get-rich-quick schemes while he slowly regained the use of his limbs. Joel and I learned that if we spent much time in the house, Dad would think of errands for us, so mostly we just hid out in the clubhouse. Then summer ended.

Life at Granite Junior High School was dog-eat-dog. Even though I was a ninth grader, and higher up the food chain, it was still miserable. I wasn't big like the jocks or especially smart like the geeks. I had acne and a bad haircut, which, when my dad got partial use of his hands back, was once again administered with his Ronco electric hair trimmer. The hoods, who gathered outside the north doors after school to smoke, took notice of me and made my life even more miserable. They tripped me, knocked books out of my hands, and generally harassed and humiliated me. And I worked at a burger place that paid sixty cents an hour and made you wear a paper cap. That time in my life nothing was worth remembering. That is, up until the day I found Grace in a Dumpster.

CHAPTER
Five

A boy found me tonight as I was looking for food in a Dumpster. He acted like he didn't know why I was in there, which makes me thinks he's either dumb or good.

✴. GRACE'S DIARY ✴.

FRIDAY, OCT. 12

About ten yards behind the Queen, on the other side of the drive-thru lane, were two small structures. One was a sheet metal storage shed where we kept supplies like napkins, cups, industrial-sized cans of tomato sauce, and the five-pound bags of spiced soybean filler we'd mix with the beef to stretch it further; the other was a walk-in freezer. My first night working at the Queen a co-worker named Dean sent me to the freezer for a bag of frozen Tater Tots and locked me inside for nearly a half hour. I think he only let me out because it got busy and he needed my help.

It was nearly eleven P.M. and the end of my shift when I went out to the shed to re-stock our shelves. With the exception of a street lamp at least fifty yards away, there was no lighting out back, and I was always a bit leery of going out there at night. Gary told me that a few years earlier one of the evening workers had been mugged by a couple hoodlums hiding out back. As usual, I looked around before I stepped out, then slid a rock under the door to prop it open. I quickly ran to the freezer, unlocked the door, retrieved a bag of lard, closed the door and snapped the padlock shut. I was walking back when I heard something. My heart froze. I looked around but saw no one. Then I heard the sound again. Some-one was definitely behind the Dumpster. No. *In* the Dumpster.

I quietly walked backward toward the Queen, keeping an eye on the Dumpster. Suddenly, a girl popped up; she was as surprised to see me as I was to see her. She was holding a hamburger, which she quickly dropped. She looked familiar.

After a moment she said nervously, "I

dropped something in here. I was just looking for it."

I realized how I recognized her; she was in my seventh period Spanish class. I didn't remember her name; she sat in the back corner of the room and never raised her hand and only spoke when the teacher called on her. I knew she was Dumpster diving but I didn't want to embarrass her.

"Do you want help finding it?"

"No, I'm okay."

She pushed herself up with her arms and swung her legs over the metal edge so that she was sitting on the flat rim of the Dumpster, then dropped down to the asphalt. She had short umber hair and beautiful large brown eyes—almond-shaped like my mother's. I remembered seeing her for the first time at school and thinking she was pretty, but then she just kind of faded into the background. She was small, a few inches shorter than me. It was hard to tell what her figure was like because she wore a coat that was too large for her, but she seemed to be more developed than most of the girls my age. She stooped and lifted her schoolbag, then flung it over her shoulder.

"You're in my Spanish class," I said.

She looked even more embarrassed. "Yeah."

"What's your name again?"

"Grace."

I was certain I'd never heard it before. "Grace?"

"Well, the teachers call me Madeline. My full name is Madeline Grace. What's your name?"

"Eric."

"Oh, yeah," she said, though I doubt she ever knew it. I could tell she was uncomfortable. I wondered if after I left she would climb back in the Dumpster to look for more food. The thought made me sad.

"We're just cleaning up. Do you want to come in and get something to eat?"

"That's all right," she said hesitantly, "I've got to go."

"You can have whatever you want. I get the food for free."

She stood there, caught between hunger and pride, her breath freezing in the air in front of her. Pride isn't worth much on an empty stomach.

Finally, she said, "Okay."

I led her in the back door past the stoves

and stainless steel food prep tables, dropping the bag of lard next to the fryer.

Dean, who had locked me in the freezer my first night, was out front mopping the dining room floor. He had turned the radio to a rock 'n' roll station and King Curtis's "Soul Twist" blared throughout the lobby. We walked around to the front.

"Hey, Dean, this is Grace. I'm getting her something to eat."

"Whatever," he said without looking up, mindlessly making wide half circles with the mop.

Grace stood at the edge of the dining area, just short of the wet tile. "I don't want to walk on your floor."

"Doesn't matter," Dean said. Dean disliked Mr. Dick and to him any job done less than the boss wanted was a victory of sorts. Then he looked up at Grace and his expression changed. So did his voice. "Don't worry about it. Really."

It was obvious that he liked the way she looked. I didn't know why, but his interest in her bothered me.

"What do you want to eat?" I asked.

She looked back at me. "I don't care. Anything would be nice."

"We have, like, everything on the planet."

"What do you like?"

"The pastrami burger, onion rings, baklava, the caramel cashew malt."

"What's baklava?"

"It's this Greek thing. It has like honey and walnuts and it's wrapped in . . . uh, paper-stuff."

"Paper?"

"Phyllo dough," Dean said. "Idiot."

I blushed a little. "It's good," I said.

She smiled. "Surprise me."

"The Eric Special coming up." *Stupid thing to say*, I thought as I walked back to the kitchen. I wondered if she could tell that I never really talked to girls. I remembered that I still had my dopey paper hat on and quickly removed it. In ten minutes I brought out a tray crowded with everything I had mentioned and a bag of Tater Tots. Instinctively, I glanced out to the parking lot to make sure Mr. Dick wasn't spying on us.

Grace looked over the tray in amazement. "Wow. You didn't have to get me *everything*."

"You don't have to eat it all."

I set the tray down in front of her. She

examined each item. "Is this the . . . bock stuff?"

"Baklava."

"I'll save that for last," she said. She took a bite of an onion ring.

I pointed to a plastic tub of sauce. "That's fry sauce. My boss invented it. It's like ketchup and mayonnaise mixed together. It's good."

She dipped the ring in the sauce, then shoved the whole thing into her mouth. "Mmm . . ." Next she peeled back the yellow wax paper from a burger. She took delicate bites at first, each bite growing larger until she was practically wolfing the burger down.

Dean moved next to her, leaning against his mop handle. "How do you and Eric know each other?"

She answered with a mouth full of burger. "We've got a class together."

"Cool," he said, which is about as original as Dean got. "So you're what, like sixteen?"

"Fifteen."

"You look like you're sixteen." I could tell he wanted to ask her out but wouldn't because I was there. Not out of respect or anything; he just didn't want to be embarrassed in case she said no. Finally he said to me, "I'm outta here. You can lock up."

"No problem," I said.

"Come around again," he said to Grace. "It's Dean."

He walked out the back door. "That's Dean," I said.

"Yeah, I got that."

"He's kind of a jerk."

She smiled wryly. "I got that too."

"I think he likes you."

"Lucky me." She started on her malt. The back door shut and Dean revved his car three or four times more than usual, no doubt trying to impress her.

"Where do you live?" I asked.

"Just west of the school."

"That's like three miles from here."

"Yeah."

"How are you getting home?"

"I'm not going home." She spun her cup, and drops of condensation gathered on her fingers, which she wiped onto the table. "I ran away." She let the cup settle. "I'm never going back."

I wasn't sure what to say to that. I remembered that I hadn't seen her in class for a few days. "How long ago did you leave?"

"Monday."

"How come you ran away?"

"For kicks."

Eating out of Dumpsters didn't look like "kicks" to me.

"For kicks?"

"Yeah. I can do whatever I want. Stay out as late as I want." She frowned. "I'm still figuring things out."

"What about your parents?" I asked.

She took a long drag from her straw. Then she said, "They don't care."

"Really?"

"My stepfather doesn't like me." She looked down at her watch, an oversized man's Timex with a Twist-O-Flex wristband. "It's late. I better go."

"I need to finish cleaning up," I said. "But you should finish eating."

"Okay."

I was amazed to see that she finished everything. She threw away her trash and stacked her tray with the others, then she walked around to the kitchen where I was wiping down the stainless steel counters.

"Thank you. Maybe I'll see you around."

"Hold on a second." I filled a large sack with the leftover food we usually threw out and handed it to her. "You can have that for later."

She looked in the sack. "Thanks."

"Where are you going now?" I asked.

She shrugged. "I don't know. I guess I'll just walk around for a while."

"It's supposed to snow again tonight."

She didn't say anything, just stood there, holding the sack of food. Maybe it was how helpless she looked or how pretty I thought she was, but at that moment I said the most out-of-character and bravest thing I'd ever said. "You could come home with me. I live about six blocks from here."

To my surprise she actually seemed to consider it. "Are your parents home?"

"Yeah," I said quickly, thinking she wouldn't come if they weren't.

She frowned. "I better not. They might call someone."

She was right about that. My parents didn't like anyone getting into their affairs and afforded others the same consideration. They'd be on the phone with her parents or the police before she got her coat off. Still, I couldn't let her freeze. Then

I had a brilliant idea. "I know where you can stay. My brother and I built a clubhouse in our backyard. It's probably cold but it's better than nothing."

"A clubhouse?"

"Yeah. It's pretty big. My brother and I slept in there almost every night last summer. It's got a mattress and everything."

"You sure?"

"Yeah."

"No one will see me?"

"Our house has five acres and it's way out back. You can't see it from the house. I don't think my parents even know it's there."

"You have five acres? You must be rich."

"Believe me, we're not."

"You *sure* your parents won't see me?"

"My dad can't walk and my mother never goes out back. It's the perfect hideout."

"Why can't your dad walk?"

"He has Guillain-Barré. It's this disease that paralyzes you."

"Wow."

"Well, they say it's not always permanent. He can walk with crutches now."

"That's good," she said.

"So are you coming?"

"Sure."

We stepped outside and I pulled the door shut, locking it behind us. A light snow had started to fall. I got my bike and pushed it beside me as we started the walk to my home. I wanted to say something clever but had no idea what that might be. The silence became uncomfortable. Fortunately Grace was better at conversation than I was.

"So, do you work every night?" she asked.

"No. Usually just three or four times a week."

"How's the pay?"

"Not good," I said. "Like almost too small to see with a microscope."

"Then why do you work there?"

"The cool hats."

She laughed.

"And I can ride my bike to work."

"That's a plus," she said.

"Yeah."

The walk home took us less than ten minutes. As usual all the lights at my house were off, except in the front room and on the porch. Still the moon was full and reflected brightly off the snow, illuminating the whole yard as if the snow crystals held radiance in themselves. I hadn't ever brought anyone home and I suddenly felt embarrassed by where I lived. A part of me wanted to just walk on by, which wasn't much of an option when you live on a dead end.

"Thar she blows," I said. I glanced over at Grace expecting a look of shock or, at least, pity, but if she felt either she hid it well. "It used to be my grandmother's house. It's kind of a shack."

"It's not bad."

She actually sounded sincere and it made me wonder what kind of a house she lived in. I stopped a few yards from our mailbox. "We'd better be quiet. Sometimes my mom sits in the front room and reads."

Grace moved close to me. We passed under the dark canopy of elm that lined our property, pressing along the edge of the driveway toward the garage, the wheels of my bike on the gravel making a lot of noise. I found a dry spot and leaned my Schwinn against the garage wall.

The snow on the yard was about eight inches deep and crusted on top, making it nearly impossible to trudge through quietly, though Grace did a better job of it than I did. The clubhouse was a dark mass in the looming shadow of the garage, its roof covered with nearly a foot of snow. I was suddenly very glad that we'd added the supporting brace.

I knelt down on one knee and brushed the snow from a chunk of granite we'd placed near the door. Underneath was a rusted key. I unlocked the padlock then pushed the door open and crawled in.

I hadn't been inside the clubhouse since the first snowfall; it smelled musty and dank. The carpet was cold and crusted with frost. I felt my way to the post in the center of the room and stood, fumbling until I found the light and switched it on. It was cold enough inside to see my breath.

Grace crawled in after me, holding the sack of food in front of her. She slowly stood and looked around the room. "You built this?"

"Yeah. My brother and me."

"It's really great."

"Thanks."

"It's purple."

"I know," I said. "My brother did it. It's the only color paint he could find."

"I like purple," she said. She glanced at the Vargas poster but said nothing. I suddenly felt a little awkward.

"That was my grandfather's," I said apologetically.

"She's pretty," Grace said. She looked at the fruit dryer. "What's that?"

"It's a fruit dryer."

"What does it do?"

I wondered if this was a trick question. "It dries fruit."

"Why would you need a machine to dry fruit? You can just wipe it off."

"No, it dries it up, like the way they make raisins from grapes."

"They make raisins from grapes?"

I wondered if she was kidding. She wasn't. "Yeah."

"Does it work?"

"Yeah."

She wrapped her arms around herself. "Maybe we could turn it on."

"It doesn't make much heat. I'm sorry, it almost feels colder in here than outside," I said. "It's like the meat locker at the Queen."

"It'll warm up," she said hopefully. "Eskimos live in igloos. It can't be *that* bad."

I pointed to the corner. "That's the mattress. And our sleeping bags." I unzipped Joel's sleeping bag and laid it across mine for extra warmth, but it was cold like everything else. I lit the kerosene lamp on the small wooden box we used as a table and the sweet scent of kerosene filled the room. The sight of the flame at least made it seem warmer.

"That will help," she said.

"I've got an idea. I'll be right back."

I crawled out the clubhouse door and ran to the house. Fortunately the back door was unlocked and I tiptoed in. My parents' room was across the hall from the one Joel and I shared and I could hear my father's heavy snore echoed by my mom's lighter snore. I softly pulled their door shut, then looked through the hall closet until I found what I'd come for. When I returned, Grace was in the sleeping bag with her coat still on. She had found our Etch A Sketch and was drawing. The bag of food was open next to her. The club-house already seemed a little warmer.

"Look at this," I said. "A heating pad." I plugged it in the opposite side of the extension cord. An amber light glowed on its control box and within a minute it was toasty warm. "Try this."

"This is great." She looked a little relieved as she put it inside the sleeping bag. "Have you always lived here?" she asked.

"No, we moved here last May."

"Do you like it?"

"No."

"What don't you like about it?"

"Everything."

"Like what?"

"Like our first week here my mom dropped me and Joel off at the movie theater. After the show a gang of kids followed us out to the parking lot. They wanted to beat us up because we were clean-cut."

"You got beat up?"

"No, but almost. My mother drove up and they ran off. But you know how it is. There's a fight at school almost every day."

"I know what you mean."

"My mom grew up here. She said Utah was a nice place to raise a family but it must have changed."

"It might just be this area. It's poor. There's a lot of trailer parks and stuff," she said. "Where did you used to live?"

"California."

"I've always wanted to go to California."

"People were nicer in California. The whole time I was there, there was only one fight at school. And it wasn't so cold there." I rubbed my nose. "What about you? You like it here?"

She sighed. "I wish we'd never come. We moved here from Hawaii."

Hawaii seemed like a foreign country to me and as exotic as any place I could imagine. "I've never met anyone from Hawaii. Why'd you move here?"

"My mother got married again. Stan said he had work here but he doesn't ever work. He just sits around and drinks beer."

"Think you'll ever go back?"

"I hope so."

"How's the heating pad?"

"It's really warm."

"Good," I said. "You can adjust it if it gets too hot."

"Thanks."

"Are you going to school tomorrow?"

"It's Saturday."

"Oh yeah, right." I felt a little stupid. "Do you want me to bring you something to eat in the morning?"

"That would be nice."

I pointed to the orange pump. "If you're thirsty, it works. Just lift the handle. There's a cup there." Joel and I had tied a string to the handle of a tin cup and hung it from the spigot.

"Groovy. It's like indoor plumbing."

I smiled. "Well, I'll go so you can get some sleep."

"Thanks. Oh, where do you . . ."

I looked at her blankly.

". . . go to the bathroom?"

I blushed. "There's an outhouse on the other side of the chicken hut. It's just a little over that way. It's kinda creepy, but it's better than nothing."

She nodded. "Okay."

"All right. Good night."

I crawled out and shut the door behind me. The snow was falling heavily now; by tomorrow morning there would be several more inches on the ground. I hoped Grace would be warm enough. At least the club-house was better than a Dumpster. As I walked back I couldn't believe a girl was living in my clubhouse. I wondered how long she'd stay.

CHAPTER
Six

Last night I slept in a clubhouse in a boy's backyard. I don't know how long I'll be here, but it's better than any of my current alternatives. And it has a transistor radio.

✷ GRACE'S DIARY ✷

SATURDAY, OCT. 13

The house was already in motion when I woke the next morning. I could smell bacon frying and I could hear my mother in the kitchen talking. I suddenly remembered Grace and felt a strange excitement.

During the summer Joel and I trapped animals in the spring box traps we found in the garage. The traps didn't hurt the animals but we quickly learned that setting them free could pose a problem, as the animals were usually in a pretty foul mood by the time we got to them. Mostly we caught rats and raccoons. One Sunday we went out to find we'd trapped a skunk. Even though it was my turn to release, I talked Joel into letting it out. As he opened the cage door, he got the full spray of the polecat's wrath. My mother made Joel bathe in tomato juice and vinegar, then she burned his clothes in the fireplace. He didn't talk to me the rest of the day, which I didn't mind since he still smelled like the skunk.

This morning I felt like I had trapped something really big in the clubhouse.

✦

I pulled on a T-shirt and Levi's and went out to the kitchen. My mom was at the stove wearing her pink flannel robe. Joel sat at the table eating.

"Good morning," my mom said cheerfully. "I didn't hear you come in last night."

"You were already asleep."

"How do you want your egg?"

"Scrambled. And may I have three eggs this morning?"

"Three?" She turned to look at me, her eyebrows raised.

"I'm just really hungry. Must be a growth spurt or something."

She began cracking eggs into a bowl. "It snowed a lot last night."

I looked out the window. The storm had dropped more than a foot of snow on the ground. I thought of the clubhouse and hoped the roof had held.

"I'm driving Dad to Uncle Norm's this morning. You boys want to go?"

"Yeah, Daddy-o," Joel said.

"Don't say that," my mom said. "It's not respectful."

"Sorry."

I didn't think he sounded very sorry.

Uncle Norm had a two-story home with a color television on each floor. Dad and Norm would sit in the two La-Z-Boy chairs and watch football while Aunt Geniel fed us. There was always lots of food: hot dogs, potato salad, and the best baked beans in the world, the kind with brown sugar and strips of bacon laid across the top. While the adults watched football, Joel and I would start up a game of Risk or Monopoly. Aunt Geniel usually baked chocolate chip or sugar cookies. As far as I was concerned, Uncle Norm's was the only good thing about moving to Utah so I surprised even myself when I said, "I'm not sure."

Joel looked at me stunned.

"I've just got some things I need to do."

"Like what?" Joel asked.

"I've got a school project, sort of."

My mother dished the eggs onto a plate. "Well, make up your mind. We're leaving in fifteen minutes."

Joel stared at me incredulously.

"I've got to tell you something," I mouthed.

"What?" he said out loud.

"Shut *up,*" I mouthed back. I stood up and walked to our bedroom, gesturing for Joel to follow me.

"What's going on?"

I glanced back to be sure our mother wasn't within earshot. "There's someone in our clubhouse," I whispered.

"What?"

"There's a girl in the clubhouse."

He shook his head. "You wish."

"Oh yeah? I'll make you a bet. Loser does the dishes for the next month."

Joel was smart enough to not take the bet, but he still didn't believe me. "Why would there be a girl in our clubhouse?"

"Is it a bet?"

"No. You're up to something."

"Come see."

"If you drop a bucket of water on my head, Mom will kill you."

"I'm not going to do anything to you."

We walked back into the kitchen to find our mother gone. As I was scooping the eggs into a bowl, she walked back in. *"What* are you doing?"

"Uh, I thought I'd eat breakfast outside."

"Just eat it in here."

"I miss the clubhouse."

"Eric, it's freezing outside."

"Please. I won't be long. Then we'll go."

She shook her head and sighed. "Just don't leave the bowl out there. And hurry. We need to leave soon." She walked back out.

I put a piece of buttered toast on top of the eggs and Joel followed me out to the backyard.

"If this is one of your stupid tricks . . ."

"Jeez, enough already. I'm not going to do anything to you."

When we got to the clubhouse I knocked on the door, then pushed it open. I got down on my knees and stuck my head in, holding the bowl of eggs in front of me. It was dark inside, and little Eva's "Loco-Motion" was playing on the radio.

"Grace, I brought you some breakfast." She didn't respond. It was much warmer than it had been the night before. I crawled in and turned on the light. She wasn't there. Joel came in after me.

"She's not here," I said.

"I *told* you no one was here. You have to do the dishes."

"No, I don't. We never bet." I looked around. "You can see someone was here. Who do you think turned the radio on? And there's her bag."

Joel seemed baffled by the evidence. "Then who is *she*?"

"A girl I met at the Queen last night. She ran away from home and didn't have any-place to go. I told her she could stay here."

Just then Grace crawled back in. "Eric . . ." She froze when she saw Joel. Joel stared back at her. I'm not sure who was more surprised.

"It's okay," I said. "He's my brother. He won't tell anyone."

She crawled the rest of the way in, then stood. "I was using the bathroom."

"How'd you sleep?" I asked.

"Pretty good. It warmed up a lot. The heating pad helped."

Joel just stared at her. Grace put out her hand. "I'm Grace."

"I'm Joel. Glad to meet you," Joel said formally, which coming from a ten-year-old sounded pretty funny.

I handed her the bowl. "I brought you some breakfast. Scrambled eggs."

"Thanks. I love eggs on toast." Grace took the bowl and sat down. She folded the toast and scooped up a clump of the eggs.

Joel asked, "Where are you from?"

"I live by Granite Jr. High."

"How long are you going to stay here?"

Even though I had wondered the same thing I still wanted to kick him.

"I don't know. A few days . . ." She looked at me. ". . . if it's okay with you guys."

"Sure," I said.

"Groovy. So what are you guys doing today?"

"We're going to my uncle's," Joel said before I could answer. "How about you?"

"I don't know. I'll probably go to the library."

Just then we heard the strained, quivering honk of the Bee. It sounded like a moose in mating season.

Grace jumped. "What was that?"

"That's my mom," Joel said.

I said to Joel, "Tell her I'll be right there."

Joel started to crawl out the door. He looked back at Grace. "Bye."

"Goodbye."

After he was gone Grace looked at me anxiously. "You sure he won't tell?"

"He won't tell a soul. Joel's good at keeping secrets. Like one time a friend of mine stole a whole bag of Hershey candy bars. Joel found out and we didn't even have to give him any to keep him from telling."

She seemed relieved.

"You sure you're okay alone?" I asked.

She nodded. "I'm used to being alone."

"What will you eat?"

"I'll figure something out."

"I'll bring you back some food tonight, just in case." The horn honked again. "I gotta go." I started for the door. "Wait, I need the bowl."

Grace dumped the rest of the eggs on the toast. "There."

"Groovy," I said.

She smiled. "Is that the first time you've ever said that?"

I felt myself blush. "Yeah."

"Groovy." Grace smiled at me.

I crawled out. "Groovy," I said to myself. It still didn't sound natural coming from my mouth.

I set the bowl by the back door and ran around the side of the house to the driveway. When I got in the Bee, Joel didn't say a word but I thought he looked at me with a new sort of respect.

✦

Our day at Uncle Norm's was great as usual. Aunt Geniel was in fine form and laid out a spread of food like none we had ever had at home, even in the comparatively fat days of California. I suppose she knew we didn't have much. She'd always say that Joel and I looked like waifs (we didn't know what waifs were except hungry) and she happily took it upon herself to fatten us up.

When my mom arrived to pick us up later that evening, I asked Aunt Geniel if I could take some food home with us. She usually sent us home with plates of food anyway but tonight I wanted to be sure. I wasn't asking for Joel and me. Even with the fun we had, I found my thoughts frequently turning to Grace. I wondered if she was cold and if she had found something to eat. I also worried that she wouldn't be there when we got back.

Aunt Geniel filled two paper platters with cold cuts, cheese, cookies, and sandwich buns, and covered it all with Saran Wrap. While my mother was talking to my aunt, I took the platters out to the van and put them in the back, covering them with one of the cushions we kept back there.

It was dark when we got home. "You boys go right to bed," my mom said. "We've got church in the morning."

"Okay," Joel said.

"Eric, give me a hand. Dad's not feeling well." My mom grabbed my dad's crutches and we positioned ourselves on either side of him as he lowered himself out of the van. When the three of us had made our way to the front door he said, "Okay, I've got it," and hobbled off to his room with us trailing behind him, just in case. He sat down on the bed and my mom took his coat and hung it along with her own.

"Good night," I said, and walked out to

the kitchen, then ducked through the back door to retrieve the two platters of food I'd left in the van. I carried them to the clubhouse. As I neared I could see several sets of footprints in the deep snow. I tapped on the wall. "Grace. It's me."

I knelt down and opened the door, then shoved the platters through the opening, crawling in after them. Grace was in the corner reading. She immediately set down her book, eyeing the food with great interest.

"I thought you might be hungry," I said.

"I'm *starving*."

I set the platters next to her and she grabbed a roll, took a bite, then tore it open. She stuffed the inside with ham, roast beef, and cheese and practically shoved the whole thing in her mouth.

While she ate I looked around. There was a pile of books next to her. "You went to the library?"

Swallowing a mouthful of food, she said, "I got some books."

I looked over what she'd taken. *The Hobbit. Black Like Me. Catcher in the Rye.*

"Did you like going to your uncle's?"

I nodded. "Aunt Geniel doesn't have any

children so she spoils us." I picked up *Catcher in the Rye.* "You know this book was banned."

"I know. It made me want to read it."

"What's it about?"

She finished her sandwich and began making herself another. "This guy who gets kicked out of school and runs away."

I could see why she got the book. I picked up *The Hobbit.* "I've read this."

"I heard it was good."

"It's really good." I set it back down. "So what are you doing tomorrow?"

"Nothing. How about you?"

"We have church. But I can get out of it. I was thinking maybe we could do something." I studied her face for a reaction.

"That would be fun."

"Okay," I said, trying not to sound too excited. "It's a date. I mean, it's not a *date,* but we'll do something."

She smiled. "See you tomorrow."

"Okay. Bye."

She waved as I crawled out.

✦

Joel was in the kitchen making himself a glass of Ovaltine when I walked back into the house. "She still there?"

"Yeah." I poured myself a glass of milk, measured in a couple heaping tablespoons of Ovaltine and began stirring, the spoon ringing off the sides of the glass.

My dad called from his room. "Hey, Eric, what did you do with that food?"

I stopped stirring. "What food?" I asked.

"The food Geniel sent home with us."

I didn't know what to say.

"You didn't forget it, did you?"

Joel looked at me. Without saying anything I pointed to the back door.

"Oh."

"Sorry," I shouted. "Guess I did."

My father groaned. "I wanted another one of those ham sandwiches."

CHAPTER
Seven

Eric saved my life today. Of course I wouldn't have been in danger in the first place if it wasn't for him, so I guess it just evens things out.

✦ GRACE'S DIARY ✦

SUNDAY, OCT. 14

As a boy I hated church. Not the institution or God, just going to the Sunday service. I believed in Jesus and I always said my prayers and grace over meals. It was just the boredom of sitting on a hard bench hearing the same thing from old people every week.

I suppose my church experience was a bit more varied than most. My parents never really settled on a specific religion. My dad always said that heaven was like a wheel and every church was a spoke leading to the same place, so with that core philosophy my parents selected their church the way most people select diners—by proximity. We had gone to Methodist, Baptist, and Lutheran churches. Since the closest church was a Mormon one about three blocks from our home we started going there.

Mormons go to church for hours on Sunday. In fact, they'd go in the morning and then they'd go back again at night. I couldn't figure out why anyone would want that much church. I did my best to survive it. Usually I'd take my pad of paper and pencils and draw a lot; that's where I decided to be a cartoonist and made up my first comic strip. But as often as not, I tried to get out of going, sometimes feigning illness. Looking back, I'm sure my mom knew what I was doing but she rarely called me on it.

A few years earlier I told her that I didn't want to go to church anymore at all. She said nothing but the look on her face was punishment enough. I'm sure it made her feel like she had failed me, or Jesus, or both of us. I spent that whole Sunday feeling guilty about disappointing my mother and in the end decided it would be less painful just to go.

My dad was pretty vocal about his belief that no one should ever be made to go to church, which was a little self-serving since he was pretty much hit-and-miss himself. After his illness he didn't go to services for about six months. When he finally did return, it was usually just a half hour or so before the hard pew became too uncomfortable for him, and we stood up as a family and left.

Joel didn't mind church. In fact, I suspect he liked it. The first week at our new church he came home with a star on his forehead for being a good boy in Sunday school. Of course I made fun of him and he never wore a star home again even though I'm sure he got more. Joel was always good.

That Sunday I decided Grace was a good enough reason to stay home. I told my mom that I didn't feel like going to church but promised I'd go next week. I waited for her face to register disappointment but for some reason it didn't. She just said, "Okay," and "C'mon, Joel."

After my mother left I got out of bed and

got dressed. I went to my parents' door and peeked in; my father was still asleep. I put on my shoes and coat, spooned the oatmeal my mother had left on the stove into a bowl, and went out back, closing the back door quietly behind me.

Grace was sitting in the corner of the clubhouse eating a cookie. The meat and cheese were gone from the platter, which amazed me since there were at least five sandwiches worth. Although she had changed her blouse, she was still in the sleeping bag and it was pulled up to her waist. She smiled when she saw me.

"Hi."

"I brought you some breakfast."

I gave her the bowl. She set down the cookie and began eating the oatmeal. It seemed like she was always hungry. I wondered if girls just ate a lot. The only female I really knew was my mother and she never ate much. "How was your night?"

"Good," she said between bites. "It wasn't too cold."

I sat cross-legged across from her. "My dad says it's always warmer before a storm. There's supposed to be another big snowstorm this week. Bigger than yesterday's."

"What day?"

"I'm not sure. I think Wednesday."

She took another bite of oatmeal. "Figures."

"Why figures?"

"Wednesday's my birthday."

"Really? How old will you be?"

"Sixteen."

This surprised me. We were in the same class and I was just fourteen.

As if reading my mind she said, "People start school later in Hawaii."

"So what are you getting for your birthday?" I asked. She looked at me with a pained expression. It was a stupid question. "Sorry."

"It's okay." She finished eating the oatmeal and handed the bowl back to me. After a moment she said, "I miss how my birthdays used to be. For breakfast, my mother always made chocolate chip pancakes. Then she would take off early from work and we'd go somewhere, like the zoo or the park." A distant look came to her eyes. "It's been a while. My last birthday she gave me a Twinkie with a candle in it because Stan was taking her away for the day. I could tell she felt bad about it. Stan plans these 'outings' whenever something important in my life comes up. It's his way of showing who's the boss. He's big on who's the boss."

"I'm sorry," I said. Again.

She looked at me and forced a smile. "But I'm here now, so I don't have to worry about that."

"You must have been real hungry."

"Because I'm eating so fast?"

"No, because the plate is empty."

"I put the cheese and meat outside in the snow to keep it cold."

"Outside?"

She nodded.

"That's not a good idea."

"Why?"

"There are a lot of animals around here. Rats and raccoons and stuff."

"Rats?" She turned pale. "I didn't know."

"Where'd you put it?"

"Just outside the door, around the corner."

I looked out. The platter was still there, but the meat and cheese were gone, and Saran Wrap littered the snow.

"Looks like they got it. I should get you a bucket or something. You could fill it with snow, like a refrigerator. That's how they used to keep things cold." I looked at her. "So I was thinking today we could go exploring."

"Where?"

"Just out back."

"Are you sure no one will see me?"

"My dad's still in bed. Mom and Joel won't be home for a few hours."

"Let's go." She climbed out of the sleeping bag and put on her coat and gloves. When we were outside she asked, "Does your family always go to church?"

"My mom always does. My dad goes sometimes. But most of the time she just takes me and Joel."

Grace thought about this. "I wish my family went to church."

This surprised me. I didn't see her as the churchgoing type.

We crossed the crusted snow of the backyard to the south end of the property.

"Did you know it snows in Hawaii?" Grace asked.

"Really?"

"Yeah. Not like this though. Just at the tops of the volcanoes."

"I'd like to see a volcano in real life," I

said. "So how come they start school later in Hawaii?"

"I don't know. They just do." She put her hands in her coat pockets.

"When's your birthday?"

"It was in May."

"What did you do for it?"

"I got that radio in the clubhouse, a couple of airplane models, and some socks. Nothing special."

"Did you do anything fun?"

"Well, my dad was just out of the hospital and we were getting ready to move, so my mom took Joel and me to Shakey's Pizza. They play banjos and organ music. It was pretty fun."

"Groovy."

I wished I could say *groovy* as naturally as she did. We walked up over a small bridge that crossed the creek and connected the street in front of our house to our next-door neighbor's place, which was set back at least fifty yards from the end of our dead-end street. The house as usual was dark and looked deserted.

"Who lives there?"

"I don't know. Some old guy with a big dog. He's pretty creepy."

"Why?"

"He never comes out. But one time Joel saw him watching us through a telescope."

"That *is* creepy."

The creek below the bridge was a wide path of ice lined on both sides by rows of river willow.

"It's kind of pretty," she said. "The way it all froze up like that. Is it safe to walk on?"

"The ice is like a foot thick. Joel and I tried to break it with a hammer but couldn't."

I walked down the side of the steep bank, slipped once on the snow but quickly regained my footing. Grace stood at the top of the bank. "I'm going to fall."

"I'll help you." I walked halfway back up and held out my hand. She took it and followed my steps down to the side of the creek. I stepped onto the ice. "See. It's like concrete."

She followed after me. "It feels solid."

She slipped and I reached out for her. Grace grabbed on to me, laughing. "It's okay. I'm just clumsy." She didn't let go of my arm, which I didn't mind. We walked down the creek toward the backyard, completely hidden to the world by the willows that grew on both sides creating an arched corridor.

"Have you ever tried skating on this?"

"I don't know how to skate."

"I do. It's fun." She slid across on one leg, the other out behind her, her arms spread wide. "Look, I'm Sonja Henie."

"I like hockey," I said. I reached in my pocket and took out a bottle cap, then dropped it on the ice and kicked it with the side of my foot. It only went a few yards before hitting the bank. Grace shuffled across the ice to where it had stopped and kicked it back. I stopped it and kicked it back to her. It went between her legs and maybe ten feet past. "Score!" I said.

"Yeah, wait until my next kick," she said, sliding back. Suddenly there was a loud crack. "What was that?" she asked.

"I don't know. Don't move." Suddenly Grace fell through the ice. The creek was only a yard and a half deep but she fell sideways, and her head went under water.

"Grace!"

She sputtered and flailed about until she grabbed on to the edge of the ice. She leaned up onto it and it broke, dropping her back in the water. I ran up the side of the bank holding on to the willow branches for support and leaning out over the water.

"Grab my arm!"

She reached over and grabbed me. I pulled her backward, falling into the bushes with the weight of our motion. Then I pulled her the rest of the way out of the water. She was shivering violently. We edged along the bank until we came to an impasse of a thistle bush.

"We need to go back on the ice," I said.

"No."

"There's no other way back. I'll go first."

I tried the ice, then I took her hand, and we stepped onto the sheet and cautiously shuffled to the opposite bank. Then I put my arm around her and helped her up the steep, snow-covered incline. When we were on solid ground I took off her coat and put mine around her. She seemed disoriented, which I knew wasn't a good thing. I had learned about hypothermia in scouting. They taught us to watch for the umbles: stumbles, mumbles, fumbles, and grumbles. Grace was stumbling and mumbling. We needed to get inside the house. My father was home but the last I saw of him he was in his bedroom. It didn't matter; she had to get inside. I led her back to the bridge. As we neared the house Grace was shaking so hard I practically had to carry her. I walked as fast as I could with nearly her full weight leaning into me. We finally got to the back porch, and I opened the door. I could hear the television; my father must have gotten up.

"Come in," I whispered.

"Is your dad home?"

"He won't come out."

Suddenly my dad yelled, "Eric!"

"Yeah?" I shouted back.

"Get me a Dr. Pepper."

"Sure. I need to go to the bathroom first." I turned to Grace. "C'mon. Hurry."

We slunk around the corner to the bathroom. I quickly turned the shower on full and steam filled the room. Grace tried to take her clothes off but her hands were trembling so badly she couldn't do it. I pulled off her coat, then knelt down and untied her shoes. When she had stepped out of them, I pulled her socks down and off. She tried to unbutton her blouse but she couldn't push the buttons through. She looked at me helplessly. I suppose this would be most teenage boys' ultimate fantasy, but I was a young fourteen and was as terrified as I was mystified by the opposite sex.

I reached my hand inside the shower. The water was scalding. I adjusted the knobs until it was warm. "Get in," I said.

". . . my clothes . . ."

"Just get in. You're already wet."

She stepped inside the shower. The first minute or so she shivered as the hot water soaked through her clothing. Then she seemed to relax.

"I'll be back," I said.

As I was shutting the bathroom door my dad called again. "Eric, where's my Dr. Pepper?"

"Coming."

I got a glass from the cupboard, a bottle opener and a bottle of soda out of the refrigerator and brought them to him. Even though much of the dexterity had returned to his hands, he was still unable to open a bottle. I pried off the bottle cap and poured the soda into the glass. "Here you are."

He stared at me. "Why are your pants all wet?"

I looked down. My pants were soaked. "I was walking by the creek and kind of fell in."

"Through the ice?"

"Yeah."

"What were you doing by the creek?"

"Walking."

He just looked at me blankly. He likely would have said more but he seemed pretty much baffled by most things I did these days. "It sounds like there's water running."

"Yeah, uh, it's the toilet . . . you know how it runs sometimes."

"It sounds like the shower."

Just then the Bee pulled into the driveway.

"Looks like Mom came home early," my father said.

Now I was worried. "I'm going to take a shower," I said. "Mom wouldn't want me to catch a chill." I hurried back to the bathroom. Grace's clothes were in a pile on the floor outside the shower.

"Are you okay?" I asked.

"Yes." She sounded normal again.

"You scared me," I said.

"Me too."

"We have a problem. My mom just got home."

She stuck her head out. "What do we do?"

"Just stay in there, I'll figure something out."

"I need some clothes."

"I'll find some."

Fortunately my mom saved my clothes after I grew out of them for Joel. I could hear my brother talking to my mother in the hall. When their voices quieted, I opened the door a crack and peered out. Joel was just a few yards away. "Hey," I called in a loud whisper.

He turned to me. "What?"

"Get me some of my old clothes from the hand-me-down box."

"Why?"

"Grace fell in the creek."

It took a moment for him to make the connection. "Is she in there?"

"Yes."

"With *you*?"

"Just get the clothes," I said. "And don't let Mom see you."

As if on cue, my mom came around the corner. "What are you doing?"

"I was just asking Joel to get me some dry clothes. I fell in the creek."

"Through the ice?"

"Yeah."

"What were you doing by the creek?"

"Walking."

She looked at me with the same blank expression my father had. Then she said, "Supper will be ready in a half hour."

When she was gone, Joel asked, "What should I get?"

"Just something warm. Not my summer clothes."

"Does she want underwear too?"

I thought about it. "I guess."

I shut and locked the door. A few minutes later Joel knocked. I cracked open the door; he was holding a stack of clothes.

"Did you get socks?"

"You didn't say to."

"Of course she needs socks. Where's Mom right now?"

"She's making dinner."

"I've got to get Grace out of here." I thought for a moment. "I need you to create a diversion."

Joel smiled and nodded his approval. He had read enough comic books that the idea of creating a diversion clearly pleased him. "I know. I'll put a dishcloth on one of the stove burners and start a fire in the kitchen. Then, while Mom's trying to put it out, you could sneak her out the back."

I looked at him. "That's the stupidest thing I've ever heard. Just ask her to help you with your homework."

"What kind of distraction is that?"

"If the house is on fire, we're all in trouble."

"I don't have any homework."

"Make some up."

The shower shut off.

"Just give us five minutes. Make sure Mom's in the kitchen. I'll take Grace out through our bedroom window."

"I can't believe you're in there with a naked girl."

"Just do it." I shut and locked the door.

"Could you get me a towel?" Grace whispered.

I took one from the towel rack and turning my head handed it around the corner of the shower. "Joel got you some clothes."

"Thanks."

"I'll just put them on the floor. You can wear them until yours are dry. My parents

think I'm showering, so I need to stay in
here. I promise I won't look."

"Okay."

A few minutes later she stepped out of
the shower. "I'm dressed." I turned around.
She looked better, though it was odd seeing her in my clothes. She looked at herself in the mirror and grinned. "I've never
worn boy's underwear before."

Joel knocked again on the door. He
held some socks. His math textbook was
under his arm.

"Hi, Joel," Grace said.

"Hi." He frowned at me. "I already know
how to do all this."

"It doesn't matter," I said. He started to
walk away. "Wait."

"What?"

"Is Dad still in the living room?"

"Yes."

"Okay. Go." We waited a few more minutes before I again peeked out the door. I
could hear my mother talking. I turned back
to Grace. She was wrapping her wet
clothes in a towel. "Let's go."

Grace followed me around the corner to
our bedroom. I locked the door behind us.
"We'll go out the window."

"What about my shoes?"

I hadn't thought about that. "You'll have to wear my snow boots. They're in the kitchen. You better hide in the closet while I get them."

She went inside, crouching beneath a curtain of hanging clothes. I shut the door and walked out to the kitchen, trying my best to look like I wasn't hiding a girl in my bedroom closet. Joel looked at me quizzically.

My mother looked up. "I thought you took a shower."

"I did."

"And you put the same clothes back on?"

"I mean, I'm about to take a shower."

I grabbed my boots and hurried past them. Fortunately my mother's attention had shifted back to helping Joel. When I got back to my room I locked the door again, then opened the closet. Grace was sitting cross-legged on the floor. "Here."

She slipped her feet into the boots.

I went to the bedroom window and tried to open it. It was stuck and it took both of us to get it open. I climbed out the window first, then helped Grace out. We kept to the perimeter of the yard and out of view of the windows until we were far enough from the house to safely cut across the yard. We were panting from the exertion when we finally got back inside the clubhouse. Grace climbed inside the sleeping bag, then lay back on the mattress.

"How do you feel?" I asked.

"Better," she said. "It felt good to shower."

We were both quiet, and then Grace started laughing.

"What's so funny?"

"Everything," she said. "I'm crawling through windows and wearing boys' underwear." She put her hand on my leg. "Are you going to school tomorrow?"

"Yeah."

"I have some things in my locker. Would you mind getting them?"

"Sure. What do you need?"

"Just bring everything. But the most important thing is a red cloth pouch. Whatever you do, don't lose it."

"A red cloth pouch," I repeated.

"You'll need my locker combination." She took a pen and a piece of paper out of her school bag and wrote it down. She

also wrote "red cloth pouch" and under-
lined it three times. "Here you go."

I folded the paper and put it in my pocket.
"I better get back inside before my mom
finds out I'm gone. She thinks I'm taking a
shower." I got down to crawl out.

"Eric, thanks for saving me."

I looked up at her. She had an expression I'd never seen on a girl's face, at least
not one looking at me. I wasn't sure what it
meant, but I liked it.

"You're my hero."

"Any time," I said.

As I walked back to the house I realized
that I really had saved her. Of course I
wasn't about to win any awards, as technically I'd put her in danger to begin with,
but when you're a fourteen-year-old boy
with acne and a bad haircut, it felt good to
be somebody's hero.

CHAPTER

Eight

Last night, Eric brought me a two-week old newspaper. There was an article about a riot that started when a negro enrolled at the University of Mississippi. It seems strange to me that we could put a man in outer space but have trouble putting a black man in college.

✦ GRACE'S DIARY ✦

MONDAY, OCT. 15

I hated being back at school, which would have been true even without having Grace in my clubhouse, but somehow her being there made it worse. The day passed at glacial speed and all day I sat, chewing on my pencil while my thoughts revolved around Grace.

Spanish was my last class of the day and for some reason I kept looking back to the corner of the room where Grace usually sat. I felt strangely important being the only one who knew where she was.

Mrs. Waller was going down the roll when she suddenly looked up. "Has anyone seen Madeline Webb?"

I looked straight ahead.

"Anyone?"

"I think she's sick," a voice said from the back of the room. "I heard she had pneumonia."

"Oh." She made a mark on the attendance sheet, put it back in her desk, and started the class.

As soon as the bell rang I set out for Grace's locker. It wasn't easy to find. It was one of a dozen lockers on an obscure row placed in no man's land. It was like the builders of the school had realized they had some extra lockers sitting around and someone said, "Hey, let's put them there."I probably wouldn't have found it if I hadn't taken a break from my search to look for a water fountain and stumbled across it.

I took the folded paper with the locker combination out of my pocket and began turning the dial. It felt a little like I was breaking into a safe. It took me a couple tries to get the door open.

Inside Grace's locker there was a mirror

taped to the inside of the door and several pictures of cheerleaders cut from magazines taped to the sidewalls. I saw a stack of folded clothes sitting on the bottom of the locker and it occurred to me that she had been planning her escape for some time. Underneath the clothes was the red cloth pouch. It was nearly as thick as a brick but flexible. I wanted to look inside but didn't. I figured if it was that important it was best I didn't know.

I collected everything inside and was stowing it all in my knapsack when someone said, "What do you think you're doing?"

I turned to see a broad girl with short brown hair. She was at least three inches taller than me and had a look on her face like she wanted to pound me into the ground and she probably could have. "That's not your locker."

"Yeah, it is."

"No, it's not. I know that girl."

I didn't know if she really was a friend of Grace's or, more likely, if the unlucky recipients of these out-of-the-way lockers all just came to know each other by circumstance, like people stranded on a deserted island.

"I'm just getting some things for her."

I slammed the locker shut, threw my schoolbag over my shoulder and walked away, hoping she wouldn't follow. She yelled something after me but that's all. I looked down at my watch. I was late for the bus. I broke into a run for the north doors, which I usually avoided because the hoods were always hanging around them. Fortunately they weren't there, but neither was my bus. I could see the last orange bus a hundred yards away from me rounding the corner of the parking lot onto Third East. I groaned. It wasn't like I could call anyone for a ride.

I had made the walk home before and vowed never to do it again. The school was about three and a half miles from our home and it took me almost an hour to make the journey. And that was without all the snow and ice. And I was wearing my canvas converse high tops.

"Dang it!" I shouted, which was about as harsh an expletive as I ever used, and started off for home. An hour and a half later I walked in our front door, my feet soaked and numb from the cold. My father was reading a book. He looked up at me. "You're late."

"I missed the bus." I wiped my feet on the scrap of carpet my mother had put by the front door. "How are you feeling?"

"Getting better," he said, which he always said.

My dad continued to look at me with a peculiar expression I couldn't read. The Bible says that the guilty flee when no man pursueth, I guess that's how I was with my secret. Had he found out about Grace? Did she leave something in the bathroom? I wondered if he was waiting for me to spill the beans, like the time Joel threw a baseball through a neighbor's window and our dad asked us everything about our afternoon—except about the broken window—until we finally caved.

"What?" I finally said.

"Look at what I'm doing."

I looked at him and still had no idea what he was talking about. "Yeah?"

"I'm reading a book."

What does this have to do with Grace? I thought. "I didn't know you couldn't read."

"Don't be a smart aleck," he said. "Of course I can read. I can turn the pages."

"Oh. That's great." I hoped I sounded excited.

"Darn tootin'." He went back to his book.

I walked out of the living room into the kitchen. Joel was at the table working on a jigsaw puzzle. He looked up at me.

"Where you been?"

"I missed the bus."

"You walked home?"

"No. I flew."

He went back to his puzzle. "Want to help?"

"No. I've got to go to work." I lowered my voice. "Have you checked on . . . ?"

"What?"

I tilted my head toward the back door. "You know."

"The girl?"

"Shhh!"

"I didn't know I was supposed to."

"She's probably hungry."

"It's like having a pet," Joel said.

I went to the pantry. I selected cans from the back of the shelf, carefully considering what I could take that my mother wouldn't miss. I grabbed a couple cans of

Van de Kamp's pork and beans, a can of Campbell's cream of chicken soup, and a can of string beans. We had an old army cooking pan in the clubhouse and I figured she could heat things over the kerosene lamp. I cut two thick pieces of my mother's homemade bread, and put it all in a brown grocery sack along with a can opener, a fork, a spoon, a plate, and a bowl. Then I retrieved my schoolbag and went out back. As I neared the clubhouse, I could smell something bad. When I opened the door the smell intensified. The light and nightlite was off. "Grace?"

She didn't answer but I could hear her lightly snoring. I thought it was a little strange that she was napping this late in the afternoon. I set the paper sack inside the door, along with the things from her locker, then rode my bike to work.

CHAPTER
Nine

Hawaii is the most isolated place with a big population on the face of the earth. It even has its own time zone. I think that's how I feel back here.

✦ GRACE'S DIARY ✦

Monday at the Queen was the slowest day of the week, but that didn't mean we had less work. Mr. Dick created what we called the Monday death list. I think he put things on there for us to do just so he wouldn't feel like we were wasting his money, like putting all the paper money in the cash register president's head up and facing in the same direction or changing the words on the sign up front.

The worst job was changing the oil in the fryer. Fortunately we didn't do it often. "Grease costs money," Mr. Dick always said, so we only changed it once a week.

He would have held out longer, but after seven days of using the same grease everything we dropped into the fryer started tasting the same, be it French fries, corn dogs, or burritos.

I was alone in the back, rolling burritos and stacking them in a plastic container when Dean came back.

Dean was a master of avoiding work. In fact he was a genius at it. I think that if he worked half as hard at working as he did avoiding it, he would have had a perennial lock on Employee of the Month.

He had two main tactics. One, he would wander around the kitchen like he was looking for something, occasionally stopping to talk to people who *were* actually doing work. When they looked like they were about to brush him off, he'd say, "I can't talk anymore, I gotta find that . . ." and he'd leave before saying what it was he was looking for.

His second trick he saved for closing time. He'd grab the mop and spend nearly an hour mopping the front dining room, a ten-minute job at best. If you called him on it he accused you of low standards of cleanliness. Whenever you had to close with him it would generally take an extra half hour to get out while you did everything yourself.

Dean jumped up on the back counter.

"So, spud, tell me about that girl."

"What girl?" I rolled another burrito.

"The one you brought by the other night."

"I didn't bring her."

"Whatever, you Pollock. She was pretty tasty."

"Yeah, well she's not your type."

"Yeah?"

"Yeah. She has taste."

His eyes narrowed. "Then why is she hanging out with a loser like you?"

"Lucky, I guess."

"You're *such* a nerd."

He went back out front. He didn't say anything else to me for the rest of the shift but he smacked me in the back of the head on his way out. I had never been happier to hear his car engine rev.

Jackie and I had the late shift. I liked Jackie. She was in my math class at Granite and was tall, wore braces on her teeth, and had bright red hair. She also played the violin and was on the chess team, which pretty much put her in the same social class as me.

She talked a lot about dumb things, like the existence of leprechauns and life on Venus, but I never heard her say a mean thing about anyone. (An interesting note: In her mid-twenties, Jackie became a female bodybuilder and was later recruited by the Women's World Wrestling Federation. Her violin lessons weren't wasted. She was called "The Maestra." After she'd pin someone she would hold them down with her foot, play Bach's "Toccata and Fugue in D Minor," then break her violin over their head.)

As we closed up I filled a bag with leftover food. I remembered how Grace had devoured the onion rings so I put a couple jumbo-sized orders inside. Jackie saw me stowing the food in my knapsack. "Mr. Dick would purée you if he saw you doing that."

"I know."

"Don't worry, I'm not going to tell. I think it's a stupid rule. Mr. Dick would rather we throw the food away then take it home. He doesn't respect us."

"Jackie," I said. "We're teenagers. No one respects us."

"True," she said sadly.

❄

After Jackie's mom picked her up, I locked the back door and rode home. My legs still ached from my walk from school and my shoes were still wet. To make it worse, the temperature had dropped into the twenties.

Once I was home I didn't even think about being seen; I went straight for the clubhouse. The light was still off inside and the things I had brought from Grace's locker were still untouched by the door. I was suddenly worried.

"Grace?"

Nothing.

"Grace, you okay?" I found the flashlight and pointed it toward the corner. She was in the sleeping bag, which was pulled up to her neck. She yawned and rubbed her eyes. "Yeah," she said, her voice weak and gravelly. "What time is it?"

"It's almost eleven."

"I slept until noon?"

"Noon? It's night."

She sat bolt upright. "I slept all day?"

"Yeah." She didn't look right to me. "What's wrong?"

"I don't feel well. I threw up."

Now I understood the smell. I turned on the light. She raised her hand to shield her eyes. "Are you sick?"

"A little."

"What do you have?"

"It's nothing. I'll be fine."

"Well, you've got to be better by Wednesday for your birthday."

Her lips rose in a surprised smile. "You remembered."

"Of course. It's an important day."

Her smile spread wider, and again she was looking at me in a way a girl never had. My face felt hot. "I got the things from your locker. I just put everything there."

She crawled over and pulled everything out until she found the red pouch. She untied it, then pulled out a large wad of bills. Not just ones, there were tens and even twenties.

I stared at it in wonder. "What did you do, rob a bank?"

"It's my stepfather's gambling money."

"You *stole* it?"

She put the money back in the pouch. "It's not really stealing."

"How is it not stealing?"

"Look, it's his responsibility to take care of me, right?"

"Yeah."

"So I'm using this to take care of me, right?" She had a point. She retied the pouch and put it in the sleeping bag. "I'm not a thief," she said angrily, though it sounded more like she was trying to convince herself.

"I'm sorry."

"It's okay. Thanks for getting my stuff. I hope it wasn't too much trouble."

I thought of telling her about my walk home in the snow and my frozen feet but for some reason I just said, "No trouble." I handed her the sack of food. "And I brought this from work. You don't have to eat it if you're not hungry."

"I'm always hungry," she said, which from what I knew of her seemed to be true. She lifted an onion ring and took a big bite out of it. After swallowing she asked, "What are you doing tomorrow?"

"Same as today. School and work."

"That doesn't sound fun."

"It's not supposed to be."

"Do you ever play hooky from school?"

I hesitated. "Sure," I said coolly. "Who doesn't?" If I sounded like the liar I was, she didn't seem to notice. The truth was I had won three awards for perfect attendance.

"Great, then let's play hooky tomorrow."

I was trapped by my own lie. The truth was I was proud of my perfect attendance awards. That sounds pathetic, but they were the only awards I'd ever received. Now I felt pressured to throw them aside like yesterday's casserole just because I didn't want to look dumb for some girl. I wondered if I got caught playing hooky, if my awards would be taken away like Jim Thorpe's Olympic medals.

Even worse than losing my awards was my terror of getting caught by a truant officer. I had never actually seen one or was even sure that they existed, but I'd heard about them and I didn't want to take any chances.

"I can't miss work . . ."

"That's okay," she said. "It's just until school's out."

"What if you're still sick?" I asked hopefully.

"I'll be okay."

I sighed. "Okay," I said. "I better go." I got down on my knees to crawl out.

"Mañana," she said.

"What?"

"Tomorrow, silly. We learned it in Spanish."

"Oh. Yeah."

I walked back to the house with dread in the pit of my stomach. If my parents ever found out I had played hooky, I was dead and buried.

CHAPTER
Ten

I met Eric's mother at the grocery store.
I think it's peculiar that she rang up my
groceries and had no idea that I was taking
them to her home.

✦ GRACE'S DIARY ✦

TUESDAY, OCT. 16

The next morning I got ready as if I were going to school. Mom made us Cream of Wheat for breakfast and, as usual, Joel put so much raspberry jam in his bowl that his cereal was crimson.

"Like a little Cream of Wheat with your jam?" I asked.

He took a mouthful, reading the back of a cereal box. "I like it this way."

"I'm going to work early," my mom said. "We're counting inventory. Want a ride to school, Eric?"

Not once since school started had my mother asked if I wanted a ride. It's like she knew I was up to something. "Uh, no. Thanks. I'm meeting someone on the bus."

She looked at me with pleasant surprise. "You have a new friend?"

My mother was always concerned over my lack of friends.

"Yeah."

"What's his name?"

"Who?"

"Your friend."

"Oh. Gra . . . ck."

Her eyebrows rose. "Grack?"

I nodded.

"That's an odd name. Where's he from?"

"Uh, here."

"Hmm. Sounds Hungarian. What nationality is he?"

"American," I said. "I think."

"Well." She looked at the clock. "You'd better get going. Maybe Grack would like to come over sometime."

"Yeah. Sure. I'll ask."

She walked over and kissed me. "Have a good day," she said and left the room.

"Who's Grack?" Joel asked.

"Who do you think?"

He put another spoonful of jam in his cereal. "I have no idea."

"That's just gross," I said.

I don't know how many lies I had told in my life but I was sure that I'd soundly trounced my record in the few days since Grace had arrived. Now I was playing hooky. I wasn't sure what power Grace had over me, but I hoped she wouldn't make me do anything worse.

I grabbed my school bag and started walking for the bus stop. My mother drove past me halfway down the street, waving as she went by. As soon as she had turned the corner I looked back down the street to see if anyone was watching (as if my neighbors suddenly had nothing better to do than to make sure I was going to school). I didn't see anyone so I turned back. I ducked into our next-door neighbor's backyard, then crawled through the hole in the fence that separated our yards. (Joel and I hadn't made the hole, but we'd enhanced it a bit.) I crossed into our backyard and knocked on the clubhouse door. "It's me."

I crawled inside. Grace watched me enter. "I wasn't sure if you were going to come or not."

I dropped my school bag on the floor. "Why?"

"You just seemed a little . . . nervous."

I was glad she hadn't said "afraid." "Where are we going?" I asked.

"The mall."

The mall? I thought. The place was probably teeming with truant officers. *We might as well play hooky in front of the school.*

The mall was a forty-five-minute walk from my house. We probably could have reached it sooner except I insisted we keep to the back roads, which Grace didn't seem to mind. If there were truant officers at the mall, they didn't see us. This made me wonder if they were just boogeymen that school administrators and parents made up to keep us in line.

We walked, unstopped, into store after store as Grace looked at clothes. For me we made a stop at a bookstore and a model shop. On the way back, we ate lunch at a diner. "Ain't you a cute couple. You two playin' hooky?" the waitress asked

"Science Fair," Grace said.

"Oh," the woman said.

I ordered a hot dog with relish and a

side order of French fries. Grace ordered a bowl of tomato soup with a grilled cheese sandwich. Afterward we each ordered apple pie à la mode.

When no one was around Grace asked, "So, do you like playing hooky?"

"Sure."

"You were afraid we were going to get caught, weren't you?"

"A little."

"Me too. But I was so sick of sitting inside all the time, I had to get out. Sometimes you just have to take chances." She looked up at a clock on the wall. "We have about an hour of school left. Anything else you want to do?"

I shrugged. "I'm fine."

"I've got to pick up some things. Do you mind?"

"No."

"Good. I'll pay for lunch. You've fed me enough." Grace brought out the red pouch and paid the check, then we started back home. On the way she said, "I need to go to Warshaw's."

I felt a wave of panic. "I can't. My mother works there."

"Oh. Will you wait for me outside?"

I thought about it. "Okay."

I sat out on the curb at the side of the store, watching shoppers come and go and praying my mother didn't come out. Grace was gone for nearly twenty minutes—long enough that I began to fear she'd been captured. I was relieved when she finally emerged. She was pushing a shopping cart with two large grocery bags. I walked over to meet her. "Is your mom really thin with brown hair that combs back like this?" She raked her hair back over her ears.

"Yeah."

"I think she rang up my groceries. She's pretty. You look just like her."

I suppose that was a compliment but I was more concerned that Grace had been seen by my mom. "We better go home," I said.

I pushed the cart to the edge of the parking lot, then we both took a bag and started walking. My bag was pretty heavy.

"What did you buy?"

"Food, mostly. I got some bread and shredded wheat and milk; it should last me for a while. I've felt bad that you've had to feed me."

"I don't mind," I said.

"You've been really sweet. You're always nice, aren't you?"

Somehow this sounded like an insult. "Not always. I can be trouble."

She grinned. "But you're mostly nice. Do you know how I know? When you first saw me eating food out of the Dumpster, even though we weren't friends then, you pretended that you didn't notice." She smiled. "Thank you for that."

"I just didn't want you to be embarrassed."

"I wish there were more people like you."

That was probably the nicest thing anyone had ever said to me. It took us about thirty minutes to get home. We carried the stuff around back. I packed her milk in the snow while she dragged the rest of the groceries inside. I climbed in after her.

"Want to play cards?" she asked.

"Sure."

We played blackjack and Go Fish for about an hour. She won most of the time and even when she didn't I had the feeling she was letting me win. Finally I said, "Do you know what time it is?"

She looked at her watch. "It's almost four-thirty."

"I've got to be at work in a half hour."

"Today was fun," she said.

"Yeah, it was."

It had been fun. But I was sure there would be heck to pay.

CHAPTER

Eleven

Hau'oli lā hānau *is Hawaiian for Happy Birthday.*

✦ GRACE'S DIARY ✦

On Tuesdays I worked the early shift, which happily meant I didn't have to close. Even better, it was payday. I was glad Grace and I had gotten food earlier, as it was far too risky to sneak any out today. Mr. Dick had come by to drop off our checks, which he always did grudgingly, and then he stuck around to make sure we were earning our wages. Just before I left I folded my check into the front pocket of my trousers. When I got home I went straight out back. Grace was reading *Black Like Me.*

"So about tomorrow," I said.

"What's tomorrow?"

I figured she just liked to hear me say it. "Your birthday . . ."

She smiled. "Can we play hooky again?"

"I better not. But we're going to have a party. What's your favorite kind of cake?"

"Chocolate."

"Chocolate it is. Anything else you want?"

She shook her head. "Just cake."

"It will be fun. I'm going to invite Joel. Is that okay?"

"Yeah."

"I mean, if you don't . . ."

"No, he's cute."

I felt a pang of jealousy. "Okay. I'll ask if he wants to come."

"I can't wait.

After a moment I said, "Well, I better get inside before my parents wonder where I am."

"Good night, Eric."

"Good night."

As I crawled out, I was thinking how much I liked the way she spoke my name. I walked along the driveway back to the front of the house and went in through the front door. My mother and father were in the living room, my mother reading *Look* magazine and my father in his La-Z-Boy watching *The Beverly Hillbillies.*

"Hi, honey," my mom said.

"Hi." I sat down on the floor next to her to watch the television. At the commercial break my mom said, "How was your day?"

My father said, "Keep it down, the Buick commercial's on."

"Sorry," my mom said.

"It was fine," I said, sotto voce.

"What did you learn at school?"

"Nothing."

This is the standard reply millions of schoolkids every day give to their parents and one that no parent has ever questioned, even though this was probably one of the few times it was technically true.

"Look at that," my father said. "Next year's Buick Electra. That is the future of the automobile." He spoke like he'd just had a religious experience, which might have been the case.

"Do you think you could cash my check tonight?" I asked my mom.

"It's too late. The bank's closed. I'll have to do it tomorrow on my lunch break. You don't want me to just put it in your savings account?"

"No."

"How come?"

"I don't know. It's just good to have some cash around."

"You've been such a good saver, don't get out of the habit."

"You should save for one of *those* babies," my father said, still ogling the Buick. "What a head-turner."

My mother shook her head.

I took the check out of my pocket and gave it to my mother. "I'm gonna go," I said.

"Do you have homework?"

"Uh, no. Not today."

I went into the kitchen and made myself a glass of Ovaltine, then headed to my bedroom. The lights were off. As I climbed under the covers, Joel, who was always asleep by eight, asked, "Where were you today?"

"Work."

"Before that."

I hesitated. "School."

"No, you weren't."

"Yeah, I was."

"Liars go to the devil."

"I'm not lying."

There was silence, then Joel's voice softened. "I'm not going to tell anyone."

I breathed out. "Okay, I played hooky. You satisfied?"

He didn't say anything.

"How'd you know, anyway?"

"I waited for you at the bus stop. I wanted to get a malt or something."

"Oh."

"You spend all your time with that girl."

"You have a problem with that?"

"No," he said.

The sadness in his voice made me feel bad. "I'm having a birthday party for her tomorrow. She wants you to come."

"Really?"

"She said so."

"I'll think about it." Neither of us spoke for a minute, then Joel asked, "Do *you* want me to come?"

"Yeah. Sure."

"I'll think about it."

"I'm buying a chocolate cake from Heller's."

"Okay. I'll think about it."

CHAPTER

Twelve

**I don't know why we're
celebrating my birthday.
It would have been
better that I'd never been born.**

✳ GRACE'S DIARY ✳

WEDNESDAY, OCT. 17

In spite of my fears, no one arrested me at school the next day. In fact, it appeared that no one even missed me. Only my English teacher, Mrs. Johnson, asked where I was. I said I was sick, which wasn't a complete lie since I had had a stomachache after lunch. (Though probably just worry-induced indigestion.) Mrs. Johnson made a sharp check in her roll book as I took my seat and didn't even ask for a note from home. I guess I just looked so squeaky-clean that no one thought I was capable of breaking rules.

My mom went to the bank on her lunch hour and left the money from my pay-check on my bed, just beating the snow-storm that completely whited out the city for about an hour. It had slowed to a gentle fall by the time I got home from school.

I got the rest of my money from the jar under my bed, then rode my bike about a mile and a half to the nearest hardware store to get Grace's present.

I had decided several days earlier what to get Grace for her birthday. It was the most expensive thing that I had ever bought. I hadn't considered how I would get it home on my bike. The box it came in was way too big to fit in my schoolbag and too bulky to hold under my arm. I had to balance it between my handlebars and straddle it with my legs. It was a miracle I made it home alive.

When I got home I stowed the box in the garage. Then I walked to Heller's, a small bakery just three blocks from our home where I bought a small round choc-olate layer cake. It was covered with dark fudge frosting and the woman from the bakery wrote *Happy Birthday* on it in red icing. She asked if I wanted to put a name on it but I said no.

I brought it home and put the cake in a travel case in the garage, then I went inside to get Joel. Not only had he decided to attend the party but he had drawn Grace a birthday card and put one of his favorite baseball cards inside. I almost said something about girls not liking baseball cards but for once I did the right thing and just kept my mouth shut. We were about to go out to the clubhouse when my mother stopped me.

"Eric, we're about ready to eat. Would you please set the table?"

"Sure. Just give me a minute."

"No, right now."

I turned to Joel and whispered, "Go tell Grace we have to eat first."

"Okay." He ran off.

I got the dishes and was setting them around the table when my mother said, "So Mr. Berg asked me if you have a girlfriend." Mr. Berg was an assistant manager at Warshaw's and the last person on the planet I would expect to show an interest in my love life.

"Why did he ask that?"

"He said he saw you outside the store with a young woman."

My heart froze. I began laying down the silverware. "Must have been someone who looked like me," I said.

"He said she was pretty."

"Then it definitely wasn't me."

My mother said, "Don't be so hard on yourself. You're a handsome young man, just like your dad. Trust me, someday you'll have to beat the girls off."

I just wanted this conversation to be over. "Sure, Mom. So, what's for dinner?"

She smiled at my obvious deflection. "Meatloaf."

Joel walked back in the back door.

"Don't track any snow in," my mother said.

"Sorry."

I looked over at him and he winked, which I knew meant "mission accomplished" but looked more like he was having a facial seizure. Joel's winks were as subtle as a diesel horn.

That night at dinner my mother recounted the earlier conversation about Mr. Berg with my father.

"I don't know why Eric doesn't have a girlfriend," my dad said as if I wasn't there. "I had my first crush when I was twelve." Then, as if this reminded him of something he said to my mother. "Hon, let's go to a movie tonight. I've got to get out of here."

"After I do the dishes."

"Let the boys do them. There's an eight o'clock showing of *If a Man Answers* at the Avalon."

"Isn't that the one with Sandra Dee?" my mother asked.

"Sure is," my dad replied.

She looked at her watch. "We'll have to hurry."

It wasn't even seven but since my father now walked about as fast as a mummy in the Saturday horror matinee movies, they always gave themselves a lot of time. They left Joel and me sitting at the table—a surprisingly convenient turn of events.

"Should we do the dishes?" Joel asked.

"Just until they leave."

I filled the sink with soapy water while Joel cleared the table.

Before they left, my mom came back to check on us. She had dressed up and she cocked her head to one side as she put on her earrings. "I'm so pleased, you boys jumped right on those dishes."

"We have homework," I said.

She looked at me as if she hadn't quite heard me correctly, which I should have expected considering how little interest I'd ever shown in my homework.

"We'll be back around ten. I expect you to be asleep before we get back."

"Okay," we said in unison.

She kissed us on our foreheads, then put on her coat. We heard the Bee crank to life and drive away, spitting gravel behind it.

"Hurry," I said. I rinsed the dishes and put everything on the drying rack. When I was finished I climbed up on the counter to reach the highest shelf where the matches were kept. My parents never actually purchased matches. My dad would just always grab a handful of free packs from diners and bring them home. I shoved two matchbooks into my pocket, then started looking for candles but couldn't find any.

Joel remembered that he'd seen some candles in the Christmas ornament box in the back room and ran off to get them. He returned with a single long white candle that tapered into a point. "It's all there is," he said.

I grabbed a cake cutter, utensils, and three small plastic plates while Joel retrieved his homemade birthday card. We put on our coats and went out to the garage.

Joel was impressed by the size of my gift. "What's in the box?"

"You'll see."

I carried the box, plates, and utensils. Joel carried the cake.

The snow had been blown in tall banks nearly halfway up the side of the clubhouse. Grace had pushed the snow away from the door to keep from being sealed inside. Outside the clubhouse, I set everything down and shoved the candle halfway into the cake. Then I knocked on the wall. "We're here."

"Come in," Grace sang.

I climbed in and Joel handed me the cake. I left the big box outside the door. As usual Grace was wearing her coat. "What a storm," I said.

"I almost got snowed in."

She stared at the cake.

"Happy Birthday!" Joel said as he crawled

in. He actually crawled right over to Grace and handed her his card. "I made you this," he said proudly. It bothered me that he'd gotten to her first.

She smiled. "Thanks, Joel." She opened his card. He'd drawn a picture of a girl in a box beneath the words, *Happy Birthday Grays.*

"That's a picture of you," he said. "Your nose isn't really that big. I just don't draw that good."

"Thank you." She opened the card. "Wow, a real Joe DiMaggio card. That's so special."

"You know who that is?" I asked.

"Of course. This is a very special card." She turned to Joel. "Thank you, Joel. I'll always treasure it." Then she hugged him.

She was just being nice, I told myself. But she looked pretty happy. Joel looked pretty happy too.

"I brought a cake," I said. I handed her the cake. "It's all chocolate. The frosting and everything. I bought it. Myself."

"Thank you, Eric."

"We could only find one candle," I said.

"Can I light it?" Joel asked.

Joel was really getting on my nerves.

"Sure," Grace said.

"Okay," I said. I surrendered a match-book.

It took him about a half dozen matches to get it done. I got more annoyed at each spent match but Grace just watched happily.

"Okay, now that it's *finally* lit," I said, "let's sing."

Joel joined in. "Happy birthday to you, happy birthday to you, happy birthday dear Grace, happy birthday to you."

Grace clapped.

"Okay," I said. "Now make a wish and blow it out."

Grace turned to me. "If it's okay with you, I'd like to look at it for a while."

"Sure. Whatever you want. It's your birthday."

She stared into the flame for a moment then said, without looking at either of us, "I can see things in flames."

After a moment I asked, "What do you mean? What kind of things?"

"I can see the future."

That was one thing about Grace: I never really knew if she was telling the truth or if she wasn't but believed that she was.

"Like a fortune-teller?" I asked.

She nodded. "Uh huh. What do you want to know?"

I felt a little funny. I remembered seeing something like this once on television. There was a proper way to phrase the question. "O, seer of the future," I said, "what does my future hold?"

Without acknowledging whether or not I'd asked correctly, she looked intently into the candle, seeming to lose herself to the flame's irregular swaying. She looked at me and said, "Someday you will be someone who is feared."

I suppose I expected about anything but that. Though I liked the idea of being feared, I didn't believe her. "You must have the wrong guy," I said. "The only thing that fears me is a donut."

"Last summer I saw a grasshopper hop away from him," Joel said.

"Enough," I said.

"The flame never lies," she said. "You *will* be feared."

"How about me?" Joel said. "Do me."

Grace gazed back into the dancing flame. After a full minute she looked back at Joel. "You are going to be someone famous. Someday people will ask for your autograph."

Joel smiled broadly. "Really?"

"Famous for what?" I asked, even more annoyed that his fortune was clearly better than mine.

"I don't know," she said matter-of-factly. "Joel, I better get your autograph now before I have to pay for it."

This is absurd, I thought.

"Okay," Joel said. Grace had a pen in her bag and Joel signed the back of the baseball card. "I'll give you all the autographs you want."

"One will be fine, thank you." She took back the pen, then stowed it with her card in her bag. "All right. I'm going to blow the candle out now," she said. "Here goes nothing." Even though there was only one candle, it took her two tries.

"Darn it," Joel said. "I'm not going to be famous."

"What I see in the candle isn't a wish," she said. "It's just what's going to happen."

All I could see was that Grace was giving way too much attention to my little brother.

"Now it's time for my present," I said.

"There's more?" she asked.

"Yeah." I climbed halfway outside the door and pulled in the box. It wasn't wrapped but I had folded its paper sack around it.

"It's really big," Joel said proudly.

"It sure is," Grace said.

"Yeah. I didn't have a chance to wrap it." I pushed the box her way. "You take it out."

She lifted the box from the bag and set it on the ground for all of us to admire. It was a General Electric brand electric space heater capable of 2,500 BTUs of heating power.

"This is for me?"

"Yeah. That should keep it plenty warm in here."

"Omigosh!"

She was clearly more impressed with my gift than she was with Joel's dumb baseball card.

"Where'd you get it?"

"Kmart. I bought it."

"You bought that for me?"

"Yeah. Let's try it." I opened the box and pulled out the heater. It was about two feet wide, two feet high, and the beige color of surgical cabinets with a chrome net face. I set it in the corner, unplugged the night-light, then plugged in the heater, turning the dial all the way to high. There was the whirring of an internal fan, then the coiled metal filaments began glowing red followed by a rush of heat. For the first time that winter the clubhouse became comfortably warm.

"That is *awesome*," Joel said.

Grace said, "I'm so happy. I'm going to take my coat off!"

Her pleasure pleased me. "It works good," I said. Joel and I took off our coats too.

I looked over at her and she was looking at me with that look again. The one that made me feel funny inside.

"You shouldn't have," she said, which was what my mother always said to my father on birthdays. "That must have cost a fortune."

I nodded. "Pretty much."

"I don't know what to say. You are the best man in the whole world." Tears welled up in her eyes as she smiled at me.

Joel looked back and forth between us. "Can we eat the cake?"

"Sure," she said.

I retrieved the cake cutter from my coat and cut three large servings. It was an incredibly perfect moment. I had the admiration of a beautiful girl *and* chocolate cake. I had never before had the former, rarely the latter, and never simultaneously.

"Ah," Grace sighed with pleasure. "This is *so* delicious."

Joel had frosting smeared around his mouth. "Yeah, this is the best cake ever."

"There's plenty," I said, feeling even more magnanimous than before.

"We need milk," Joel said.

"I have milk," Grace said. She crawled out and brought back the milk we'd packed in the snow. Grace poured the milk in the tin cup, which we passed around, and then we all had seconds of the cake. Nothing had ever tasted that good to me before.

"Hey," said Joel, "what has two humps and lives at the North Pole?"

"I give up," Grace said.

"A lost camel."

It wasn't much of a joke, but for three kids high on chocolate cake it was like the atom bomb of jokes. Grace laughed so hard that milk shot out of her nose, which made us laugh even harder.

This launched a competition as we each tried to better the last joke. We were laughing so hard that we were crying and Grace kept saying, "I'm going to wet my pants."

I don't know how long we'd been out there; hours I think. Long enough to finish off the cake. That night the clubhouse was the best and happiest place on the entire planet.

Finally we ran out of jokes and our laughter faded. "We better go before Mom and Dad get home," Joel said. Grace and I just looked at each other. "Well, I'm going," he finally said. He got down on his knees and crawled out.

"Thanks for coming, Joel," Grace called after him. "And for the nice gift."

"I better go too," I said. I knelt down at the door.

"Wait." Grace put her hands on my cheeks. "Thank you, Eric." Then she kissed me on the mouth. Not a short peck like one from my mom or Aunt Geniel, but a real kiss that lasted more than ten seconds.

It was the first time that I had ever been romantically kissed. It was even better than the chocolate cake. When we finished kissing we just looked at each other. I probably looked dizzy. She just looked happy. "This was the best birthday I've ever had," she said.

"Me too," I said. She laughed and it was soft and sweet like a wind chime.

"I'll go now," I said.

She smiled. I think she was pleased to have so disoriented me. "See you tomorrow."

I got back down on all-fours. "Bye."

"Good night."

Joel was still waiting for me outside the door. When we'd taken a few steps he asked, "How much was that thing you got her?"

"Twenty-seven dollars."

"That's a lot of money."

"Yeah." I put my hands in my pocket. "Did you see what she did?"

"What?"

"She kissed me."

"On the mouth?"

"Yeah."

"Whoa!"

"Yeah," I said. "Whoa."

He looked down as our boots left deep impressions in the snow. "Was it worth twenty-seven dollars?"

I smiled. "Sure was."

CHAPTER

Thirteen

A guy on the radio said there was a ninety percent chance that we wouldn't be here in the morning.

✦ GRACE'S DIARY ✦

MONDAY, OCT. 22

Monday started out bad and deteriorated so rapidly that I shouldn't have been surprised that the day ended with the threat of total global annihilation.

Between first and second period the hoods locked me in my locker. I was in there for nearly twenty minutes before a passing custodian let me out but not until he'd delivered the obligatory lecture.

Then as I went into class, my math teacher stopped abruptly in the middle of his lecture and told the whole class to turn and look at me. He said that since I had disrupted the entire class with my tardiness I owed them all an apology and an explanation of why I was late, which, of course proved to be of great amusement to my fellow students. I would have liked to have pointed out to my teacher that the only reason there was a disruption of his class was because he stopped teaching in order to embarrass me but I knew how far that would get me. Probably to afterschool detention.

Never believe things can't get worse. At lunch I slipped on a slick of water in front of the whole cafeteria. My tray flew up in the air, and I ended up wearing most of my lunch. As was customary at Granite, everyone applauded. I ducked out of the lunchroom to clean the spaghetti sauce off my shirt. So not only did I get humiliated in front of the entire ninth grade but I didn't have anything to eat either.

When I got home from school my mother was waiting to take Joel and me to see the dentist, who discovered three cavities in my molars, which prompted a ten-minute lecture on proper dental hygiene. We got home just in time for me to hop on my bike and ride to work.

✦

When the universe has conspired to create the perfect, crappy day it only reasoned that I would be scheduled to work with Dean.

Around ten o'clock a wino stumbled in. Which, since the Queen was located just off State Street, was a fairly common occurrence. They usually just asked for a glass of water, grabbed a handful of soda crackers, then asked if we had any extra food lying around. Mr. Dick had made it very clear that we would be fired if we gave food to "hobos and other vagabonds." "Give them food," Mr. Dick said, "and those people will flock to the Queen like seagulls to a landfill."

This man didn't ask for anything. He was holding a brown bottle and staggering a little. I suppose he just wanted an audience. Dean and I had started closing. I was in the front wiping off counters while Dean mopped.

"Hey, buddy. You hear the news?" he said, a broad smile revealing gaps where his teeth were missing.

"What news?" Dean asked without looking up.

"This is the end."

"The end of what?"

"Everything!" He began laughing as he stumbled back out the door.

"Bum," Dean said.

＊

Twenty minutes later Dean, still mopping, said, "Hey, corndog, doesn't that skuzz bucket out there belong to you?"

I looked out. To my embarrassment, the Bee was in the parking lot. I walked to the door, wondering what it was doing here.

"Better tell your mom to move it. Dick told us to throw away all the trash in the parking lot."

"Shut up," I said.

My mother had climbed out of the van and was walking toward me. I unlocked the door and opened it, preferring to meet her away from Dean. She wore a grim expression.

"What's up, Mom?"

"You need to come home."

"I can't. We're not done yet."

"It doesn't matter, you need to come

home. Now." My first thought was that she'd found Grace.

"Have you heard the news?" she said.

I shook my head.

"I'll tell you when we get home. Is there anyone else here?"

"Dean."

She stepped inside. "Dean, I'm Eric's mother. I'm taking Eric home with me. You need to go home too."

Dean just held the mop handle and stared, not sure what to make of her. "We're not done. We'll get in trouble if we don't finish."

"Trust me, it doesn't matter. Just get home as soon as you can."

"What's happening, Mom?"

"Just come." I followed her out to the Bee. She wasn't crying but she was close.

"I brought my bike . . ."

My mom drove around the side of the Queen, and we put my bike inside the van. On the way home she said, "I love you, Eric." Something about the way she said it frightened me.

When I got home Joel was still up. Joel was *never* up past 8:30. He was sitting in the living room across from my father. Obviously whatever was happening was really bad. I was even more afraid.

My mother sat down between Joel and me. My dad began talking.

"Tonight, President Kennedy said on the television that the Russians have been sending atom bombs to Cuba. The Navy has been ordered to stop all Russian ships sailing to Cuba. What this means is, there could be a war."

I looked back and forth between my parents. "You mean with atom bombs?" I asked.

My dad nodded. "It looks like it."

Like all kids of our generation, we knew about atom bombs. We were practically experts on them. In school we watched black and white films of mushroom clouds and nuclear winds and pictures of smiling adults walking quickly and in an orderly fashion to fallout shelters. We had been religiously schooled in bomb drills, climbing under atom-bomb-resistant desks with our hands laced securely over the back of our necks. There were bomb shelters in every neighborhood. The possibility of a nuclear holocaust was just something we carried around in the back of our minds, like an overdue library book.

In a bizarre way, we thought atom bombs were kind of cool. They were a gift of modern technology, like color TV and frost-free refrigerators, and in those days anything modern was good. Even if it could kill you.

People would even drive to the Nevada desert to watch the underground bomb tests and would joke about who was the most radioactive. Looking back, we were just nuts. We were like toddlers playing with a grenade. I'm amazed civilization survived.

As my father spoke, Joel's eyes grew wider and wider. Even he had seen pictures of explosions from atom bombs. He'd even seen films of hydrogen bomb explosions like the one at Bikini Island, which, by contrast, made the atom bomb look like a firecracker.

"We're going to have a family prayer, then I want you to go to bed," my dad said.

"Can I sleep with you?" Joel asked my mother.

"Of course." She looked at me. "Eric?"

"I'm okay," I said.

We knelt down and prayed. Afterward

my mother reminded us to brush our teeth, which, under the circumstances, seemed absurd but, in a way, hopeful. We hugged, then I brushed my teeth and went to my room alone. I turned off the light and crawled in bed waiting for my parents to go to bed so I could tell Grace. My mother came in and sat on the side of my bed. "Are you afraid?"

"Yeah, a little."

She leaned over and kissed me. "President Kennedy will take care of us," she said. "He has children too."

As soon as my mother left and I heard her door shut I went to the bedroom window and climbed out. I ran to the clubhouse and knocked on the wall. "Grace."

She turned on the light as I climbed in. "What's wrong?"

"It's really bad," I said. "President Kennedy said on TV that the Russians have atom bombs in Cuba. There might be a nuclear war."

She stared at me. "Is that for real?"

"Yeah. My mom and dad told us, and they looked really scared. Here, you can hear for yourself." I turned on the radio. At first there was just a blast of static. I ran my finger over the plastic knob until I heard talking. A couple of men somberly discussed President Kennedy's address. We listened for about five minutes. As they spoke, Grace looked more and more afraid. I turned it off. We were both quiet for some time.

Finally she said what we were both thinking. "I don't want to die."

"Me neither."

"It's so unfair. We didn't do anything. We're just kids and we might die because of something we have nothing to do with."

We were both quiet and the only noise came from the heater.

"I don't think we're going to die," I said. I didn't sound very convincing. I wondered if it had been such a good idea to tell her. Maybe it would be better if none of us knew. There would just be a big flash and before you could say, "What was that?," you'd be gone. Maybe that wouldn't be so bad.

"If we do die tonight," she said, "I don't want to be alone." She looked so frightened and vulnerable. "Will you hold *me*?"

I put my arms around her and she laid her head on my shoulder. After five minutes or so I turned off the light. The glow of the heater bathed the room in amber radiance. We lay back on her mattress and I held her until she fell asleep.

In the middle of the night I woke to her talking in her sleep. She was crying, "Please don't, I don't like that. That hurts." Tears were streaming down her face.

I gently shook her. "Grace, it's okay. You're dreaming."

She stopped and opened her eyes and for the longest while just looked at me. Then she snuggled her head into my chest and went back to sleep.

I don't know how long it was that I just looked at her. She was so beautiful. I gently stroked the hair back from her forehead. Then I kissed her and pulled her into me as I fell back asleep.

✦

I woke before Grace did. The dawn light was stealing through the cracks around the clubhouse door. It was another half hour before Grace's eyes fluttered and opened. She looked at me, then brushed her hair from her face. "We're still here," she said.

"Yep." Then I realized we were still here.

"What if my mother's looking for me? She'll *kill* me."

Grace lay her head back on my chest. "Just tell her the truth."

"Are you crazy?"

"Not about me. Just tell her you slept in the clubhouse because you thought it might be safer."

"But that's stupid."

"No mother would ever get mad at her kid for that."

I don't know how Grace knew these things but I figured she was right. She usually was. I kissed her on the forehead. A few minutes later I crawled out of the clubhouse and made my way back to the house.

CHAPTER

Fourteen

We survived the night, but the news reports say that it's not over. It's like taking a Band-Aid off slowly.

✦ GRACE'S DIARY ✦

TUESDAY, OCT. 23

Joel was in the bedroom getting dressed when I climbed back in through the window.

"You been out back?"

"Yeah."

He didn't say anything.

"Are Mom and Dad up?"

"Mom is."

I walked out to the kitchen. I soon learned that the crisis wasn't over. That morning Khrushchev had a message for

President Kennedy. It was printed in large type in the morning newspaper:

I hope that the United States Government will display wisdom and renounce the actions pursued by you, which may lead to catastrophic consequences for world peace.

With the fate of humanity lying in the balance we went to school. Maybe half the kids stayed home; even some of the teachers didn't come. I suppose Joel and I went to school just because we always did. We had to do something. My mom still had to work. In fact the store was even busier than usual because people were stocking up on staples.

That night, Grace, Joel, and I listened to the radio and played Chinese checkers in the clubhouse.

CHAPTER

Fifteen

I once caught a moth inside our house. I took it outside and tried to release it into its natural habitat, but it didn't want to leave the box. Finally I shook the box until it fell out.

I wonder if that's what death is like.

✶ GRACE'S DIARY ✶

WEDNESDAY, OCT. 24

Two days after Kennedy announced the blockade, two Soviet ships, flanked by a nuclear submarine, had moved within a few miles of the U.S. flotilla. It was a global game of chicken with the whole world watching and wondering who would turn first.

By that afternoon no Soviet ships had crossed the blockade but twenty-three missile sites in Cuba had become fully operational. An American U2 plane was shot down over Cuba and the pilot was killed. Fidel Castro seemed to be the loudest and brashest of the leaders involved in the conflict, not surprising since he held the littlest stick. The Soviets were eerily quiet.

Every time we heard a plane we looked up and hoped that it had wings.

✳

In chess there are more than a trillion ways to play the first ten moves. I suppose there were even more possibilities of how the crisis would play out. The next days passed in a kind of surreal slow motion. Suddenly, everyone was an expert on nuclear armaments. People talked openly and knowledgeably about isotopes, point zero, radioactive fallout, and, in general, death.

America had about nine times as many bombs and missile warheads as the USSR: twenty-seven thousand to three thousand—enough bombs to kill the Russians thirty times over. The Soviet Union only had enough nuclear missiles to kill us all just once, which, frankly, wasn't very comforting. The Soviet missiles weren't as accurate as ours so to compensate for this they created bigger bombs like the Czar,

a fifty-megaton monster that would swallow entire cities, the largest nuclear weapon
ever exploded.

The one thing on everyone's mind was
whether this would be their last day alive. I
suppose that's not necessarily a bad thing.
For once we didn't worry much about the
unimportant things—just family, friends,
and God. And Grace.

✦

Friday night, I asked Grace if she wanted to
go home. Her eyes filled, but she replied,
"No."

CHAPTER

Sixteen

I still believe in prayer.

✦ GRACE'S DIARY ✦

SUNDAY, OCT. 28

They say there are no atheists in foxholes. On Sunday, six days into the crisis, Americans flocked to churches. While our country was praying, President Kennedy and U.N. Secretary-General U Thant reached an agreement with the Soviets. Khrushchev agreed to dismantle the missiles in Cuba in exchange for a no-invasion agreement and a secret removal of the Jupiter and Thor missiles in Turkey. The news flooded the airwaves and the world breathed a collective sigh of relief.

✳

People celebrate in different ways. Some people lit firecrackers. Others honked their horns or clanged pans. Up and down our street there was no sign of life. It's probably the one place on the planet that an atom bomb blast might have gone unnoticed.

CHAPTER

Seventeen

Today I asked Eric to be my boyfriend.
I know it's supposed to be the other way
around, but he's shy and it would probably
take a hundred years otherwise and by
then I might change my mind.

✦ GRACE'S DIARY ✦

MONDAY, OCT. 29

As intense as the last days had been, it was surprising how quickly everything returned to normal. It was like a near miss at a traffic intersection; everyone just keeps on driving.

As I was walking to my fourth period art class the principal's voice blared over the school's P.A. system.

"Attention, faculty and students, your attention, please. This is Principal Allen. We have a missing ninth-grade student. If you know anything concerning the where-abouts of Madeline Webb or have seen her in the last two weeks, please report immediately to my office. Thank you."

I always thought that Principal Allen's bass voice echoing down the school's tile hallways sounded like the voice of God, but this time his words actually sent shivers through me. I felt as though I was wearing a T-shirt that said, I KNOW WHERE SHE IS. I avoided eye contact with everyone in the crowded hallway as I made my way to my next class.

⋇

Later that afternoon, Mrs. Waller started off Spanish class by saying, "This has been a trying time for all of us, and many of you missed class last week. Considering the nature of the crisis our country was facing, I think it's understandable. As such, no one will be penalized for their absence."

The class erupted, especially the basketball players on the back row who, for the most part, had taken the opportunity to skip school and were now slapping and ribbing their friends who had come.

Mrs. Waller loudly cleared her throat. "Back to order, class." She waited until the classroom settled. "Thank you. Also, I'm sure you all heard Principal Allen's announcement about one of your classmates, Madeline Webb. If anyone has seen Madeline or knows where she is, please see me after class."

I'm sure it was my imagination, but it seemed like her gaze kept returning to me. I probably looked terrified or guilty or both.

"All right, let's get back to work. Turn to page one hundred and seventeen in your text. Today we are studying the adverb *where*." While I was frantically flipping through the pages of my textbook, Mrs. Waller walked from the blackboard to the center of the room near my desk. "*¿Dónde estás*, Eric?

I looked down at my book then back at her. "Uh, I'm here."

A few students laughed.

"Yes, I can see that. Now please answer in Spanish."

I blushed. "Sorry. *Yo, aqui.*"

"*Muy bien*. Eric, can you say, 'Where is Madeline?'?"

After a moment I said, "I don't know where she is, ma'am."

This time everyone in the room laughed. "No, I want you to say in Spanish, 'Where is Madeline. *¿Dónde está Madeline?*"

"Oh." I turned crimson. "*¿Dónde está Madeline?*"

"Muy bien."

I was glad when the bell rang.

※

As soon as I got home I went straight to the clubhouse. Grace had been painting watercolor pictures of flowers. I had no idea where she had acquired the painting supplies, but I didn't ask.

"Everyone at school's looking for you," I blurted out.

She looked at me calmly. "What do you mean, *everyone*?"

"Principal Allen made an announcement. Mrs. Waller even talked about you in class."

"You didn't tell anyone where I was, did you?"

"No."

"Then what's the problem?"

"What if someone finds out?"

"How will they find out? I'm in a clubhouse in a field behind your house."

"But what if they do?"

"It's no worse than if I go back."

"But, if they find you . . ."

She looked at me with sudden understanding. "Are you afraid for me or for you?"

I hesitated. "Both."

"Well, you don't have to worry about me. I can handle me."

The conversation wasn't going the way I had hoped. "The question is," I said, failing to conceal my exasperation, "when are you going back to school?"

She looked at me as if I were stupid. "Never."

"What?"

"I can't go back. If I go back, my parents will find me."

"But you can't just skip school."

"Why not?"

I had never questioned this before. "Kids go to school. It's what they do."

"Why?"

"To learn things."

"Why? So we can learn how to make atom bombs and kill ourselves faster?"

"No. So we can improve our lives."

"Right," Grace said sardonically. "My mom graduated from college, and it didn't do her any good. In fact, I think school makes you dumber."

As a three-year recipient of the perfect attendance award, I took offense to this. "How could learning things make you dumber?" I said. "That's just stupid."

"I didn't say 'learning,' I said 'school.'"

"It's the same thing."

"No it's not. School makes people lazy. They stop thinking things out for themselves and just plug in the facts other people want them to think."

"Like what?"

"How about what really happened to the Indians?"

I didn't know how to respond, since, frankly, I wasn't sure what had happened to them.

"We need school to learn socializing skills."

"What *socializing skills* has school taught you?"

She had a point. The only social lesson I had learned at Granite was that big dogs eat small dogs; a particularly disturbing lesson when you're a small dog.

"You're just parroting the Establishment," Grace said.

I was starting to get mad. "I'm not parroting."

"Yes, you are. They can tell you anything and you'll just believe it."

"Give me one example," I said.

"Okay. In Christopher Columbus's time, why were people afraid to sail?"

"Everyone knows that," I said. "It's because they thought the world was flat."

"You're sure of that?"

Her saying that made me not so sure. "Yeah . . ."

"Guess what year the first globe was invented?"

"I have no idea."

"Fourteen ninety-two. You know the poem, *In 1492 Columbus sailed the ocean blue.* It was the same year Columbus sailed. If they thought the world was flat, why were they making globes?"

"You just made that up."

She shook her head. "No, I didn't."

I couldn't tell if she were making this up or if she really was a lot smarter than me. The latter seemed likely. Either way I was losing the argument. "What does Christopher Columbus have to do with you living in my clubhouse the rest of your life?"

She looked at me, stunned. "Fine," she said between clenched teeth, then began grabbing her things and shoving them in her bag.

"What are you doing?"

"You want me to go? I'll go."

"I didn't mean that."

"Yes you did."

Even though she was turned from me, I saw her furtively wipe a tear from her cheek. I touched her shoulder. "Grace . . ."

She pulled away from me. "Don't touch me."

"Please, stop."

"No."

I grabbed her arm. "Grace. I never want you to leave. You're the only good thing in my life."

She stopped, then turned back and looked at me. Her face was streaked with tears. "You mean that?"

"Yes."

She brushed her cheeks with the back of her hand. We just sat there looking at each other, then she leaned forward and kissed me for the second time. It made me feel better.

"I better go," I said. "I have to go to work."

"Every time I kiss you, you say you have to go. Should I not kiss you?"

"No."

"No, I shouldn't kiss you, or no, I shouldn't *not* kiss you?"

I was thoroughly confused. "You should kiss me."

"Are you sure?"

"Yeah. I just haven't done a lot of it. I'm probably not very good at it."

Her eyebrows raised. "No, you're a pretty good kisser."

"Really?" I felt myself blushing.

"Really." She smiled at me. "Have you ever had a girlfriend before?"

"I had a crush on a girl last year."

"What happened?"

"Nothing. I never told her I liked her."

"You're kind of afraid of girls, aren't you?"

I didn't answer.

"A little?"

I felt stupid. "Maybe a little."

"I think that's sweet." She took my hand. "Do you want to be my boyfriend?"

I kept looking at her, waiting for the punch line. "What exactly does that entail?"

"Well, for one thing, you can't have any other girlfriends."

Fat chance of that, I thought. "That's no problem. Anything else?"

"You can kiss me anytime you want."

"Are you serious?" I asked, barely concealing my excitement.

She laughed. "Yes."

I couldn't believe it. I felt like I'd just been given a key to an ice cream parlor. "Like, I could kiss you right now?"

"Yes."

I just stared at her.

"So?" she said.

"What?"

"Are you going to kiss me?"

"Oh. Yeah." I slowly moved forward to put my lips on hers. Even though we'd already kissed twice, up to this point she'd pretty much done the heavy lifting. This was a first for me. I was as awkward as a nurse giving her first shot.

"You're not going to hurt me," she said.

Our lips touched and she closed her eyes. It was incredible. It was like Christmas, my birthday, and scones for dinner all rolled into one. When we finally parted there were big smiles on both of our faces.

"See, you are good at it," she said.

"Yeah," I replied, slightly breathless. "Let's do it again sometime."

She laughed. "Sure. That is, unless you still want me to leave."

"I never want you to leave," I said. "You should never leave."

"Then," she said coyly, "I shouldn't go back to school?"

"School makes you dumb," I said.

She grinned. "You better go. You have work."

"Right. I'll see you after."

She cocked her head. "Bye, Eric."

"See ya later."

For the first time in my life I was smitten, dashed on the rocks of femininity. I had just been given permission to kiss the most beautiful girl in the world. It was better than winning the lottery.

CHAPTER

Eighteen

There are times I feel like shouting my feelings to the entire world. But I think they'd only close their windows.

✦ GRACE'S DIARY ✦

One Sunday a minister in a small, pious community decided to play hooky from church and go golfing instead. He was afraid of being caught, so he changed out of his Sunday clothes, put on sunglasses and a hat, and quietly slipped out the back door of the church.

As he drove to the golf course, the voice of God spoke to him. God warned the minister that if he played golf on the Sabbath he'd be cursed. But the minister had made up his mind and went anyway.

The minister got to his first hole and hit

the ball. It sailed all the way to the green and bounced in for a hole-in-one.

"Incredible!" shouted the minister.

He went to the next hole and hit another hole-in-one.

"Fantastic!" cried the minister.

The exact same thing happened on all eighteen holes. "A perfect game!" the minister shouted. As he carried his clubs back to his car he looked to heaven and said, "God, I thought you said you were going to curse me. Instead I shot the best game in history!"

"Yes," replied God. "But who are you going to tell?"

That's exactly how I felt about having Grace as a girlfriend.

CHAPTER

Nineteen

The newspaper said that we need to inspect our Halloween candy because some people have put razor blades and something called LSD inside. I can't figure out why someone would do that. They must hate themselves.

✦ GRACE'S DIARY ✦

WEDNESDAY, OCT. 31

Every Halloween my mother made an enormous cauldron of chili and a couple pans of hot Parker House rolls that Joel and I would consume smothered in butter and honey. Those were good times. Part of that tradition was my mother saying, "Where are you boys putting all that?" and her favorite, "You must have hollow legs." We were never quite sure what that meant.

After dinner my parents retired to the living room for television and candy bowl duty, while Joel and I suited up in our Halloween costumes.

Oddly enough, Halloween costumes were the one thing we had plenty of. My mother liked to sew and back when she stayed home she made us new costumes every year. She even once helped make costumes for a school play I was in. We saved them all.

Joel went as the Lone Ranger complete with mask, bandanna, a cowboy hat with a drawstring, and a cap gun. I went as the devil with a red cape, a long tail, and horns. We had a pitchfork too and even though it looked cool, I wasn't about to lug that around all night.

After we were dressed we went out back, taking chili and rolls for Grace, as well as all the costumes we thought might fit her. She devoured the chili and rolls as happily as we had. Then she began trying on the costumes, eventually settling on a clown outfit my mother once wore. It was a little big on her, but no one would notice. That's kind of the point with clown costumes.

She put on a red foam rubber nose and a bright orange wig and she lined her mouth with a wide swath of lipstick. She decided to be a sad clown, so she drew tears on her cheek with eyeliner. When she was finished, I couldn't have picked her out of a police lineup.

"You really can't tell who I am?" she asked.

"Nope," said Joel.

I shook my head. "Your own mother wouldn't recognize you."

It was hard to tell with all the makeup but I think she frowned when I said that.

✦

We decided that we would go for an all-time candy harvest record. With ambitions as high as ours, we'd have to go some distance to find fertile ground—someplace far away from our poor, stingy street.

We were discussing the positives and negatives of taking our bikes when Grace said, "I know the perfect place. But we'll have to take the bus to get there."

Joel and I were open to going any place that promised more candy. I got three pillowcases from the linen closet, then the three of us walked down the street to catch the bus.

The bus ride was only fifteen minutes

long and our destination turned out to be as fruitful as Grace promised. It was a crowded suburb of small, tidy homes built close together, just ripe for the picking. There were scores of children out and the streets looked like an elementary school Halloween parade.

The three of us swept the streets with remarkable efficiency. For the first two hours we rarely even had to say"trick-or-treat," as invariably someone would already be at the door dispensing candy to another group of children.

As evening fell, the crowds started to thin, and by ten o'clock most of the little kids had gone home to bed. We continued to add to our haul, carrying our bulging pillowcases over our shoulders like Santa Claus. Although it was a reasonably warm night, relatively speaking, we still had to wear coats over our costumes.

We had worked our way over by my school when Grace led us down a small, dead-end street with pumpkins smashed in the middle of the road. The houses were smaller than the homes on the other streets we'd been to and not as well cared for. A couple of the homes had dilapidated cars parked in their front yards, with flat tires or wheels missing altogether.

"This doesn't look like a good street," Joel said. "Let's go down a different one."

"I second that," I said.

Grace continued on as if she hadn't heard us. She walked past several homes then stopped at the edge of the yard of a small bungalow. The home was pretty much the same size and construction of the other houses on the street, but it was in even worse shape. The yard was engulfed by orange-berried Firethorn bushes that also spilled over and poked through the front and side chainlink fence. One of the windows was broken and was covered with a sheet of plywood held in place with duct tape.

The sidewalk in front of the home hadn't been shoveled but had been tramped down, probably by earlier trick-or-treaters.

There was a motorcycle and an old red Ford pick-up truck in the driveway as well as another pick-up that was hoisted up on cinder blocks.

Grace just stared at the house. The curtains over the picture window were drawn but a light was on and I could see the silhouette of a woman moving around inside.

"Do you know who lives here?" I asked.

She didn't move.

"Grace?"

She turned to me with a peculiar look in her eyes. "This was my house."

My heart raced. "You shouldn't be here."

She just turned back and looked at the house. "Would you ring the doorbell?"

"What?"

"Please."

I glanced back at the house then again at her. "Are you sure?"

"I want to see my mother."

Joel stood next to me silently staring at the house. I could tell he was afraid. I suppose I was too. I took a deep breath. "All right. Come on, Joel."

We went to the front gate and opened it then marched up the walk. There were no pumpkins or Halloween decorations but I didn't think the house needed them. It was kind of scary already.

"Trick or treat," I yelled. Joel said it too, but almost inaudibly.

After another minute I went to ring the

doorbell but it was covered over by duct tape on which was written "Doesn't work." I knocked instead. I was glad when no one came and was ready to go when I heard footsteps. The door opened. A balding man stood in the doorway. He was taller than my dad, and had a large belly. He wore a white sweat-stained sleeveless T-shirt and his pants were secured by suspenders. He held an open can of beer.

"Trick or treat," I said.

He looked me over. "Well if it ain't Scratch himself." He looked at Joel. "Who are you, Howdy Doody?"

"I'm the Lone Ranger," Joel said.

He looked back at me. "Guess that makes you Tonto, sweetie." He punctuated his remark with a swig from his can. Even if I hadn't already known who he was I wouldn't have liked him. He looked out across the yard where Grace had been. I panicked.

"Are you going to give us candy or not?"

He looked back at me. "Oh, a smart aleck. Show me a trick first. That's the deal, ain't it?"

"No," I said.

"No trick, no candy."

I heard a woman's voice. "Quit giving them a hard time Stan."

He looked at me. "You think *you're* the devil?" He laughed. "Here's a trick for you. Get on all-fours and bark like a dog. Go on."

I turned. "C'mon, Joel, let's go."

"Oh, don't like that, huh?"

We walked away.

"What a couple of Marys," he yelled after us. He laughed, then slammed the door.

"I told you this was a bad street," Joel said.

When we reached the sidewalk Grace was gone.

"Where'd she go?" Joel asked.

"I don't know." I was sure she'd be waiting for us. When we got near the end of the block we found her sitting on the curb behind a garbage can. She was sobbing so hard she could hardly catch her breath. I knelt down next to her. "You okay?"

It was a while before she could speak. "Let's go home, please."

I helped her to her feet and we all walked five blocks to a bus stop. Grace didn't say a word until the bus came and we were safely on board.

"Was that your stepfather?" I asked.

She didn't answer.

"We didn't like him either."

She didn't say anything the rest of the night. She didn't even want her candy.

CHAPTER
Twenty

Last night I saw Stan. I don't know
why God put people like him on this earth.
Maybe for the same reason He made
rattlesnakes, cancer, and earthquakes.

✦ GRACE'S DIARY ✦

MONDAY, NOV. 5

Another Monday at the Queen. I was standing up front at the cash register when a woman about my mother's age walked in. She had a bouffant hairdo that looked like it was a yard high and pretty eyes that matched her blue topaz necklace. In one hand she held a rolled-up poster.

"May I help you?" I asked.

She said with a slight southern accent, "I'd like to speak with your manager."

"Our assistant manager's here," I said. "I'll get him." I walked to the back where

Gary was checking receipts against a cash register tape. "Gary, there's a woman up front asking for you."

He looked up, his eyes wide with fear. "Is she like five foot tall with kind of ratty red hair and painted-on eyebrows?"

"No."

"Good." He exhaled. "What does she want?"

"How should I know?"

"You didn't ask?"

"I'm a fry cook, not a receptionist."

"You're getting mouthy these days," he said. "Tell her I'll be just a minute."

I walked back out. "He'll be right with you."

"Thank you."

The woman picked up an Amway brochure, then slowly paced around the lobby until Gary arrived. From the way he looked at her it was obvious he liked what he saw. "Can I help you?"

She recognized his interest and her voice became honey-sweet. "I sure hope so. I'm Cindy." She extended her hand. "It's a pleasure to meet you."

Gary reached out, eager to take her

hand. "Pleasure's all mine," he said, wide-eyed.

"So you're the man in charge here?" She was working him like a rented mule.

"Yes I am."

Right, I thought.

"I'm from the Granite PTA. You've probably already heard that one of our students is missing. Would it be permissible to hang a poster in *your* establishment?"

Gary just stared at her. I could guess at the battle going on in his head between a request from a pretty lady and the grief Mr. Dick would give him. Mr. Dick would say something like, "What do you think we are, the flippin' post office?"

The blue eyes won out. "Uh, sure, miss. Just put it on that wall above the newspapers."

"Thank you kindly."

As she walked to the wall, Gary leaned over to me. "If Mr. Dick asks, I didn't know about this."

"Sure," I said. *What a pansy.*

The women took out a Scotch tape dispenser and set it on a table. Then, as she unrolled the poster she turned back.

"Would one of you gentlemen mind giving me a hand?"

Gary just stood there.

"I'll help," I said. I walked around the counter.

"Now if you'll just hold it up," she said, "I'll tape the corners."

She lifted the poster. Below a black and white image of Grace in thick block letters, it read:

MISSING
MADELINE WEBB
SIXTEEN-YEARS-OLD
Last seen at Granite Jr. High
If you have information regarding her
whereabouts please contact the police.

It seemed to me an eternity before the woman had the thing hung. The tape got caught on the spool and it took her forever to find the end of it. All the while I stood there face-to-face with Grace. Of course the woman had no idea that she was being assisted by one of the only people in the world who knew where Grace was. When she finally got all four corners taped up, she thanked me and turned back to Gary. "Thank you, sir."

"You betcha. Anytime."

The woman walked out with Gary's gaze following her every step of the way. After she drove off he walked out and looked at the poster.

"What school do you go to?" he asked.

"Granite Junior."

"Do you know that girl?"

"I had a class with her."

He shook his head. "Her poor parents must be crazy with worry."

"Mr. Dick will probably go bananas when he sees that," I said.

"Probably."

"Maybe I should take it down."

Maybe it was the lingering memory of those eyes, but to my surprise, Gary chose that moment to grow a backbone. "No. We should leave it up. It's the right thing to do."

"I don't know, Gary. You really should pick your battles."

He looked at me quizzically, no doubt wondering what had gotten into me. "I'm glad I'm not one of your schoolmates."

※

Dean came into work about an hour later. I hoped he wouldn't see the poster but, of course, it was the first thing he noticed.

"Hey, corndog, you see that poster out there? That girl looks just like the paper shaker you brought in."

"No she doesn't."

"It looks *exactly* like her. What did you do, kidnap her?"

"My friend's name is Grace. Not Madeline."

This stumped him. "Well, you have to admit she looks like her."

"No, I don't," I said.

"You're such a ditz," Dean said and he went back up front.

That night I closed with Jackie. While she was mopping up the back I went out to the lobby and took down the poster. I rolled it up and hid it up front until Jackie left. Then I put it in my coat and rode home to show Grace.

✴

"I feel like a criminal," Grace said, staring at the poster.

"You're kind of famous," I said.

"I wonder who told the PTA."

"Probably your parents."

"My mom might. Stan wouldn't. He's glad I'm gone."

I looked at her. "What if he's not? I mean, maybe you got him wrong."

She looked at me and there was darkness in her eyes. "No, I didn't get him wrong."

CHAPTER

Twenty-one

There was an article in the newspaper about me. I wish everyone would leave me alone, not so much for my sake as Eric's. He's very afraid.

✴ GRACE'S DIARY ✴

TUESDAY, NOV. 6

The next morning Joel and I were eating our Malt-O-Meal cereal when my father hobbled into the kitchen and sat down at the table. My mother handed him a cup of Postum, then left the kitchen to get ready for work. Dad poured some milk into his cup and stirred until his drink turned the pale color of caramel.

Then he casually began sifting through the stack of mail on the table. When he got to the electric bill he stared at it almost as intently as Joel had stared at the Vargas poster the first time he saw it. "Holy cow."

Joel and I looked over at him.

"Our electric bill went up nearly ten dollars. You boys need to start turning the lights off. You think money grows on trees?"

"No, sir," I said.

"Joel?"

"No, sir." Joel turned and glared at me.

My father pushed aside the mail and started reading the paper. After a few minutes he looked up. "Here's something for you, Eric. Do you know a girl named Madeline Webb?"

I looked up at him. "No, sir."

"Hmm," he said. "It says here she goes to Granite Junior. You're in ninth grade, aren't you?"

"Yes, sir."

"You sure you don't know her? She's in your grade."

I shrugged.

Joel furtively glanced at me, then put more strawberry jam in his Malt-O-Meal.

"Look, here's a picture of the girl." He turned the paper around to show me. It must have been an old picture of Grace.

Her hair was shorter now and she'd gained some weight.

"Oh, her."

"Then you do know her?"

"She's in one of my classes."

He turned the paper back around. "This article says her parents think she's been kidnapped."

"Why would they think that?"

"Because she's been missing for days," he said sardonically.

"I mean, maybe she ran away or something."

He looked up at me. "If she ran away she would have left a note or packed a bag."

I took a couple more bites of my cereal while my dad moved on to the sports section. "Tex Clevenger retired from the Yankees. Might as well go out on top. Joel, don't you have his card?"

"Yes, sir."

"I guess eight years is long enough to throw a ball around."

When I finished my cereal, I asked, "Could I take that page?"

Without looking up, my father asked, "Which page?"

"The one with the article about the girl at my school."

He handed me the local section.

"Excuse me," I said. I carried my bowl and the newspaper over to the sink. As I rinsed out my bowl Joel joined me.

"Thanks for getting us in trouble," he said.

"You don't know it's the heater. Besides, she'd freeze to death without it."

"Yeah, and now she's in the paper. Someone's going to find her and we'll be dead."

"No one's going to find her and I'm the one who's dead, not you." I rolled up the paper. "I'm going to show her the article."

I said goodbye to my parents, grabbed my schoolbag, and went out the front door. But once outside, I doubled back and ran to the clubhouse. As I opened the door I could hear music coming from my transistor radio.

"She-e-e-e-e-e-e-ry babe-e-e-e-e-e-e-e . . ."

I crawled inside, a little winded from running. "Grace."

She raised her hand. "Wait, I love this song. It's The Four Seasons."

I waited for the song to end. *"Come, come, come out tonight . . ."*

When it was over she turned to me. "Okay, what?"

"You're in the newspaper." I unfolded the paper and read, "Middle School Student Missing. Madeline Grace Webb, daughter of Stan and Holly Webb, has been missing since October eleventh."

"Let me see."

I handed her the paper.

After she finished reading the article she dropped it on the floor. "I hate that picture of me."

"There's a lot of people looking for you."

She did her best Cagney imitation. "They'll never take me alive, copper . . ."

I picked up the paper. "I'm glad you think it's funny."

"Stop worrying so much. Everything will work out."

"How do you know that?"

"I saw it in the candle."

"You did?"

She nodded.

I had no rebuttal to that. "Okay, I'm off to school."

"Say hi to everyone for me."

I turned back.

"Just kidding."

As I walked to the bus stop all I could think about was how I hoped the candle was right.

CHAPTER
Twenty-two

**Eric couldn't see why it's important
for me to keep a diary.
Maybe I just want to leave some
evidence that I existed.**

✦ GRACE'S DIARY ✦

"I'm kind of like Anne Frank," Grace said as I crawled through the clubhouse door. She was sitting in the corner holding a small, yellow vinyl book with a locking strap.

"What?" I said, instead of "who?," which was appropriate since I had no idea what she was talking about.

"Anne Frank."

I nodded as if I understood. "Does she go to Granite?"

Grace laughed. "She was a Jewish girl who hid from the Nazis during the

Second World War. Didn't you read the book?"

"No." I had never heard of it.

"They were going to send her family to one of those death camps, so they hid in the back of a building. She kept a diary the whole time. Just like me."

"You keep a diary?"

"Every day." She held up the yellow book.

"What do you write in it?"

"Whatever I feel like writing."

"Like what?"

"Things I did. People I talked to. Stuff like that."

"Am I in there?"

"Of course. You're all over the place."

"Can I see?"

She looked incredulous."No. You don't just show someone your *diary*."

"Then who do you write it for?"

"Yourself."

"That's dumb. You already know every-thing that happened to you. It's like telling yourself a secret."

". . . and people can read it after you die."

"What good is that?"

She frowned. "Maybe it will give someone hope."

I guess I was just too selfish to think of
that.

CHAPTER
Twenty-three

They say that following the path of least resistance makes rivers, and men, crooked. I suppose that's why there's so many crooked rivers and men.

GRACE'S DIARY

As I look back, I realize just how much things have changed since those days. America was a different place. More private. Children were considered the property of their parents and what happened in someone's home was no one's business but theirs—not the school's, not the neighbors', not the church's, and especially not city hall's.

While we lived at my Grandmother's house there was a family across the creek from us. The Williamses. They had, I think, twelve or thirteen kids. I was never really sure how many; counting them was like counting fish in a pet store tank. Biggest family I had ever seen.

The kids, singularly and collectively, were meaner than wolverines. It seems that at least one of them got in a fight at school every day, though oftentimes with each other. Teachers at Granite used to say, "Someone needs to discipline those children," but I don't think that was the problem. Their dad taught Sunday school at the church we went to. His pet sermon was that if you spared the rod, you would spoil the child, as if anyone wanted his advice on child rearing.

I think Mr. Williams spoiled his children with the rod or belt or whatever else he could get his hands on when the spirit moved him. The Williams children would come to school with more bruises than a two-week-old banana. I figured their fights at school were just their way of making everyone else look, if not feel, like them.

The only time my father ever beat me was when I was eleven years old and we were still living in California. One summer my mother's cousin from Phoenix came to stay with us. She had two of the most obnoxious boys I'd ever seen. Our parents were visiting and so they told us to go outside and play. Joel and I took them out to play basketball in the driveway. They shoved and pushed a lot. Then one of them tripped Joel on purpose. Joel hit the concrete and skinned up his knees and palms badly enough to draw blood. Joel was only seven at the time and he started to cry. I was already mad at the boys for tripping Joel, but then they started teasing him for crying. Before I knew it, I punched the older of the boys right in the nose. He let out a yelp as blood ran from both his nostrils.

"You're gonna get it," his little brother said. "We're gonna tell." Then the two of them scurried inside to tattle.

Two minutes later my mom stormed out of the house. I was sitting next to Joel helping him brush gravel from his knee. I assumed she would take my side when she heard the whole story. Heck, I thought she'd reward me for standing up for my brother. Instead she dragged me by my arm into the house. Once inside, my dad took off his belt, something I'd previously only heard about, and whipped me on the backside five times. I can still remember each stroke. Then my parents made me apologize. I had never been so glad as when their station wagon pulled out of our driveway. I don't remember who I was more mad at, the boys or my parents.

CHAPTER

Twenty-four

I sense that the hourglass is emptying.

✴. GRACE'S DIARY ✴.

The next month passed like a dream. I suppose this happens in most relationships, but Grace and I had settled into a routine, almost like a married couple. With all the publicity, Grace was no longer safe walking outside in daylight. Even the library had posted a "missing girl" poster on their front door.

The thickness of her red pouch had dwindled and I had to start bringing her food again. I sneaked food from home or the Queen when I could, but I was also spending much of my paycheck feeding her. I knew Grace felt bad about this. She apologized and thanked me, usually in the same breath. And while she wasn't eating as much as she had when she first came, she still seemed to be gaining weight.

During the day Grace spent her time reading, listening to the radio, and writing in her journal, but mostly just waiting for me to get home from school or work.

Her routine necessitated a change in my schedule as well. On the nights I worked I would come straight home, tell my parents good night (if they were still awake), then slip out my bedroom window.

We held hands and took long moonlit walks either on our street or in the sur- rounding neighborhoods. We talked about things I still think about today. Grace had a wisdom about life that far surpassed mine. On one of those walks we talked about love.

"Do your parents love each other?" she asked.

"Yeah. I think so. They still fight some- times, but they always make up."

She pondered my reply then asked, "Have you ever been in love?"

"I don't know," I said softly. "How do you really know when you're in love?"

She stopped walking and smiled at me. "When you don't have to ask."

✦

I never told her, but I knew in my heart that everything was moving toward some kind of flashpoint. I didn't know how or when it would arrive, but it was coming. I could feel it, like the tremor of a distant approaching freight train.

One evening we walked about a mile to a small park just east of Seventh and Forty-fifth. There was no one there but us. The trees were barren and the ground covered with snow. We sat on a bench and Grace lay her head in my lap, looking up at the stars.

"What am I going to do?" she asked.

I didn't answer because I honestly had no idea. "Where's your *real* father? Won't he help?"

"I don't know who he is. He was gone before I was born."

"Do you have any other family?"

"I have an aunt in Denver. But my mom got in a big fight with her."

"About what?"

"I don't know. My mom just said my aunt's awful and she'll never talk to her again as long as she lives."

I ran my fingers through her hair. "Maybe you'll have to go back," I said.

She just closed her eyes. I knew she never would.

CHAPTER
Twenty-five

I think the secret to a happy life is a selective memory. Remember what you're most grateful for and quickly forget what you're not.

✧ GRACE'S DIARY ✧

WEDNESDAY, NOV. 21

I don't remember everything about that time. Like most memories, the good times fade while the hard times remain sharply chiseled on the tablets of our hearts. One of those times was the day before Thanksgiving when Grace got sick.

I had just gotten home from school and went back to the clubhouse to find the light off. The heater was on high, bathing the room in bright orange light. The clubhouse felt like a sauna.

"Grace?"

She moaned softly.

I crawled to her side. "Are you okay?"

"I don't feel well." Her speech was slurred.

"Are you sick to your stomach again?"

She shook her head. "This is something different."

I leaned over and felt her forehead with my cheek like my mother always did when I was sick. "You're really hot."

"My chest hurts. I think I have pneumonia."

The word scared me. In California one of our neighbors died of pneumonia. "You're going to have to see a doctor."

"I can't."

"But pneumonia's *serious*. You could die."

"He'll just give me pills. Do you have any pills?"

"What kind of pills?"

"Penicillin. Penicillin cures everything."

"Maybe my dad has some. He has all sorts of pills. I'll go see."

I ran back to the house and went to my parents' bathroom. Rooting through their medicine chest I found an amber bottle with penicillin. I pulled off the cap. There were only two pills inside. I was pretty sure she'd need a lot more than that. I took the pills and a damp washcloth out to her.

"We only have two pills. But I think I know where I can get more." I filled the tin cup with water and helped Grace sit up. She took both pills, then lay back down. I draped the wet washcloth across her forehead. She closed her eyes and fell back asleep. I sat by her for the next hour, then went back to the house.

I found Joel laying out baseball cards into fantasy baseball teams.

"Grace is really sick," I said. "We need to get her some penicillin."

"Where do we get that?"

"Mrs. Poulsen."

"That mean old lady down the street?"

"Yeah. Old people always have pills. When we were cleaning her garage I used her bathroom. There were pill bottles all over the place. She must have like a million things wrong with her."

"That old bat won't give us any pills."

"I know. We'll have to take them."

Joel's face showed sudden excitement. "You mean we're going to break in?"

"No, she'll let us in."

"Why would she do that?"

"We'll go shovel her walk, then I'll ask to use her bathroom. When I get inside, I'll take them."

"I don't want to shovel her walk."

"It won't take long, and then we won't be stealing the pills because she'll owe us."

"She *already* owes us."

"I know, but *she* doesn't think so."

"Well, I'm not going to shovel her walk."

"Joel, we have to get those pills. It's a matter of life and death."

He shook his head and sighed, like he always did whenever I coerced him into something, which was a fairly regular occurrence. "All right."

We put on our boots and coats and carried our shovels down the street to Mrs. Poulsen's house. Even though it was only a few minutes past five the sun had already begun to set. As we shoveled we made as much noise as possible so Mrs. Poulsen would come outside. Still, it was at least ten minutes before she walked out on her front porch.

"That is so sweet of you boys. Would you like some hot cocoa?"

This would be easier than I thought. "We

sure would," I said. I set down my shovel and started for the door. The storm door slammed before I reached it.

A few minutes later she came out with a couple mugs. "Cocoa break."

Joel and I put our shovels down and took a mug.

"Could we please go inside?" I asked. "It's pretty cold."

"Let's just stay on the porch. I don't want you tramping snow inside."

Joel took a drink of the cocoa and grimaced. I took a sip. It tasted like someone had dipped a brown crayon in hot water, then served it in an unwashed coffee cup. There was a ring of lipstick on my mug.

Mrs. Poulsen stood on the porch with her familiar look of magnanimity. "I'm surprised your folks let you out after dark. Did you hear about that girl who was kidnapped?"

"Yes, ma'am."

"It was in the *Eagle.* The article said she went to Granite. Don't you boys go to Granite?"

"I do. But I don't think she was kidnapped. She probably just ran away from home."

She shook her head. "That's even worse. Worrying her folks and everyone else like that."

"Maybe she had a reason," I said.

The old lady turned on me, displaying a ferocity I wouldn't have guessed she possessed. "What reason could that awful girl possibly have to hurt her poor folks like that? Kids today don't care about anyone but themselves."

My temper flared. "She's not awful. You are."

Her mouth opened so wide that I thought her dentures might fall out.

Just then Joel handed me his mug. "I've got to use the bathroom," he said and without waiting for permission ran into the house. Mrs. Poulsen was too stunned to stop him. About five minutes later he came back out. Me and the lady were still glaring at each other.

"Let's go, Joel."

"Yes, you bad boys go on home."

"You're a mean old lady," Joel said. "And you're cheap." We stepped off the porch and he turned back again. "And your hot chocolate stinks!"

When we were back home I turned to Joel. "That was bad."

"I told you she was mean."

"Any luck with the pills?"

Joel nodded. "Got them."

"Let me see."

He pulled the bottle from his coat.

I read the label. "This is Librium."

"What's that?"

"I think it makes you happy."

"Happy pills?"

"Yeah. We needed penicillin."

Joel put the pills back in his pocket. "I'm keeping them anyway. Mom could use some of these."

THURSDAY, NOV. 22

The next day was Thanksgiving, and fate played us a winning hand. We put on our Sunday go-to-meeting clothes and went to Uncle Norm's for dinner. Before we left I went in and checked on Grace. She looked about the same, though she thought the pills I gave her were helping. I kissed her on the forehead and told her I'd bring her back some leftovers, which we both agreed were even better than the actual dinner.

✳

Thanksgiving dinner was to Aunt Geniel what the Sistine Chapel was to Michelangelo. We've all seen magazine pictures of Thanksgiving feasts with large, perfectly browned turkeys and shiny, butter-basted rolls. Then we learn the photographer's tricks, like using shoe polish to burnish a raw turkey, making it look perfectly roasted, or adding marbles to soup to make it appear chunkier.

Aunt Geniel made things that were both picture-perfect *and* edible. That year we enjoyed an amazing feast. There was spiced roast turkey, giblet brown gravy, mashed potatoes, candied yams, green beans, honey-glazed baby carrots, Parker House rolls, herbed apple stuffing, cranberry and orange relish, rice pudding, and pumpkin pie.

While everyone was eating dessert, I went in the bathroom and looked inside Aunt Geniel's medicine cabinet; there were two full bottles of penicillin.

The labels on the bottles said to take one pill four times a day for ten days. I did the math: four times ten was forty pills, minus the two I'd already given her. I needed thirty-eight pills.

I poured the entire contents of one of the bottles into my hand. There were twenty-four pills. I counted the pills from the other bottle. There were only nine. I was five pills short. But Grace wasn't very big, so maybe they'd be enough. I poured them all into one of the bottles and shoved it into my trouser pocket. I returned the other bottle to the cabinet then decided that I better take the empty bottle as well. I put it in my other pocket then returned to the table. I hated stealing something from Aunt Geniel's house, but I was certain that she would give the pills to me if she knew what they were for.

We didn't leave until around eight, when my mother announced it was getting close to Joel's bedtime. Aunt Geniel loaded us down with enough leftovers that I knew Grace's share wouldn't be missed.

✴

That night I brought Grace the pills and two large plates of food. She made a turkey roll sandwich with cranberry sauce. As good as the food was, she didn't have much of an appetite. She ate a little, then we both lay back together on the mattress. Holding her was my favorite thing in the whole world.

"Do you know what I'm most grateful for this Thanksgiving?" she asked.

I had no idea. "What?"

"You."

I smiled. "I'm grateful for you too."

We just lay in happy silence. After a few minutes, she rolled over to look at me. "So I've been thinking. Do you believe there's a hell?"

"Sure. Doesn't everybody?"

"Well, what if this *is* hell, but we just don't know it?"

"That's crazy. Hell is like lakes of fire, and there are devils with horns and pitchforks. There's none of those around here."

"But what if hell's not really like that?" Grace asked.

"Everyone says it's that way," I said.

"I don't think Jesus ever talked about fire and brimstone."

"Then why do they teach us that at church?"

"To scare us."

"Why would they want to scare us?"

"I don't know. I just don't think God wants us to do good things because we're scared. I think he wants us to do good things because we're good."

I thought about it. "You're talking gibberish," I said.

She sighed. "Yeah. Maybe I'm just sick."

CHAPTER

Twenty-six

I wonder how much longer it will be before Eric learns the truth about me.

✦ GRACE'S DIARY ✦

SATURDAY, NOV. 24

By Saturday evening Grace was feeling a lot better, and her appetite had returned. After my parents went to bed, I raided the refrigerator and brought out a plate of cold tuna casserole. I was amazed at how quickly she devoured the food. When she was done I asked, "Do you want more?"

She looked embarrassed but nodded. I went back inside and filled another plate which she downed nearly as fast. Afterward we held hands and went for a short walk up and down my street. When we got back she said, "Do you have any rubber bands?"

"A million of them." I wasn't exaggerating by much. My father had spent years making a rubber band ball that was now nearly as big as a softball.

"Would you get me a couple?"

"Sure. Now?"

"Please."

I ran inside the house and returned with a dozen or so elastic bands. She looped one through the buttonhole of her pants and secured the other end around the button. She sighed. "These were getting too tight."

"Maybe you shouldn't eat so much," I offered.

She looked stricken. "Maybe *you* shouldn't be so rude."

I frowned. "Sorry."

She sighed. "I'm sorry too. I'm just upset."

"About what?"

She looked at me and squinted. "Nothing. Just a girl thing."

I nodded without understanding. She might as well be a space alien for all I knew about "girl things."

CHAPTER

Twenty-seven

Eric said they talked about me on the television last night. It's curious. I'm much more important missing than I ever was in person.

✦ GRACE'S DIARY ✦

MONDAY, DEC. 17

It was the only Monday night of the month that I'd had off. Jackie needed some extra cash for Christmas and asked if she could work for me, and I was only too happy to oblige. That night our family sat around the television set. My dad was in his La-Z-Boy watching the news and my mother was knitting. Joel and I were locked in an intense game of checkers, oblivious to the television until the newsman said, "The hunt goes on for a missing Salt Lake girl. Madeline Grace Webb, a student at Granite

Junior High, has been missing for more than sixty days. Police suspect foul play and are currently investigating several leads, but are asking for your help. There's a five-hundred-dollar reward for any information leading to her whereabouts. You may contact the Salt Lake police directly or call this station for further information. In other news . . ."

I looked back at Joel. He was scared. Five hundred dollars was a fortune. Everyone would be looking for her.

"That's the girl from your school," my father said.

"Yeah," I replied, stiff with panic.

"Oh, my. They still haven't found her?" my mother said, her needles crossing and clicking rhythmically. "What is this world coming to?"

"Don't worry, they'll find her," my dad said. "Or at least the man who took her. They found Dillinger, didn't they? And when they do . . ."

Joel looked at me.

"What do you think they'll do to him?" I asked.

"Who knows? The electric chair's too

good for people who steal children. I'd just hate to be him."

I felt light-headed. "May I have an Oval-tine?" I asked.

"Sure," my mom said.

I walked to the kitchen, then slipped out the back door, running to the clubhouse. I quickly crawled inside. "Grace!"

Grace was curled up in the corner read-ing. "Hi," she said happily, setting her book in her lap. She saw the distress on my face. "What's wrong?"

"You were just on the television."

"Honest?"

"Well, not you. But they were talking about you. And they showed a picture of you."

Grace didn't share my excitement. "So."

"The man on the news said that you've been kidnapped and the police are look-ing all over for you. They put out a five-hundred-dollar reward."

"Well, you know I wasn't kidnapped."

"This is really serious. You were on *tele-vision.*"

She lifted her book and started reading again.

"Didn't you hear me? *Television!*"

"I heard you. I just don't care."

"You don't care? People think you were kidnapped. Or maybe dead. This is *really* serious."

"It's always been *really* serious."

"You think this is fun," I said. "It's time you did the right thing."

"And what is that?"

"Not worrying everyone."

Grace wore a dark, angry expression. "You still don't know, do you?"

"Know what?"

"Why I ran away."

I didn't know I'd missed something. "You said it was for kicks."

"And you believed me?"

"Why wouldn't I?"

Grace's eyes narrowed. "You are *so* gullible. You live in this world where you think that deep down inside everyone means well and monsters are make-believe. It's not true. People aren't all good. And there really are monsters."

I was confused. "Monsters? You mean like Dracula . . ."

"No!" She threw her book against the wall. "You're so stupid."

Her words stung. "No I'm not."

"Don't you know why I've been throwing up and why I'm getting fatter? It's not because I'm sick or eating too much. It's because I'm expecting!"

"Expecting what?"

"I'm pregnant!"

The word stunned me. In those days "pregnant" wasn't a word that even adults used casually. "How can you be . . . ?" I choked on the word. ". . . you're not even married."

She groaned. "That's what I'm talking about. You're so naive. Don't you even know where babies come from?"

"I know . . ." I suddenly made the connection. "Who?"

She didn't speak for a few moments; then she started to cry. She said, "My stepfather made me."

I stared at her in disbelief. "Your stepfather?"

She was crying so hard I could barely understand her. "If I'm sent back home, something really bad will happen."

I felt sick for drawing this out of her. I felt sick for my youth and for my stupidity. And I was aching from all the mean things she had said to me. Half of me wanted to hold her, the other half wanted to run. She continued to sob.

"He's a very bad man. He told me that if I ever told anyone what he did to me he would hurt me and my mother. He said no one would believe me anyway. And you know what? They won't. They always believe the adults."

I tried to absorb everything she had told me. Finally I said, "I believe you."

"I know you do. But you believe everything everyone tells you. You're just a boy."

This was the most hurtful of all the things she said. I looked away from her. "I guess I am. Well, I better go."

"Eric?"

I couldn't answer her; the lump in my throat was too big. I crawled out of the clubhouse without looking back. I heard her calling after me as I walked back to my stupid house finally sure of exactly who I was. I could pretend all I wanted but in the end I was still just a stupid, gullible, naive boy.

CHAPTER

Twenty-eight

I broke my best friend's heart only to learn that it was really mine.

✦ GRACE'S DIARY ✦

TUESDAY, DEC. 18

Morning fell like a sack of concrete. My head ached and I had a sick, tight sensation in my chest akin to panic. All the good feelings I'd had over the last weeks were gone. It was the last day of school before Christmas break, a half-day, and something I'd looked forward to for weeks. Now I didn't care. I didn't have anything to look forward to. I told myself that I wished she were gone. I don't know if I meant it, but that's what I told myself.

I went to the kitchen and made Grace

toast with butter, and put it and a banana inside a brown paper lunch sack. I walked out without my coat. I didn't knock, just opened the door and tossed the sack inside like I was feeding an animal at the zoo. "Here."

Grace had been waiting. She stuck her head out the clubhouse door. "Eric, can we talk?"

"No." I turned.

"Please, don't go."

I walked away.

"I'm sorry I was so mean." She started to cry. "Please, Eric. Please, talk to me."

I kept walking until I was nearly to the edge of the yard.

She yelled after me, "Okay, I'll leave. You'll never have to see me again." She stopped, overcome with emotion. "But I have to say something to you. Please," she sobbed. "You're all I have."

I stopped and turned back. "What do you want?"

Grace climbed out of the clubhouse and scrambled to her feet. It was the first time in more than a month that I'd seen her outside in the daylight. I could see how much her figure had changed.

"I'm the stupid one, not you. I hate myself. I just want to tell you I'm sorry from the bottom of my heart. I'm sorry I said you were just a boy. You're not. You've been brave and kind and good. All you've done is protect me and take care of me and that makes you more of a man than any man I've ever met."

I didn't say anything.

"I'm so sorry. I'd rather face my stepfather than hurt you again."

I stood looking at her, her nose wet with snot, her eyes red and swollen. I exhaled, then spoke in a normal voice, "Get back inside, someone might see you."

"I don't care. You're the only one in this world I care about. If I don't have you I don't care what happens to me anymore."

I walked back to her. "Don't say that."

She shook her head. "I mean it." Then she said in a lower voice, "I cut myself for you."

"What?"

"I cut myself for you." She lifted her arm to show me. There was a mass of blood dried to her forearm.

I gasped. "What happened?"

"I punished myself. I wanted you to see how bad I felt."

"That was stupid," I said, crouching down to gather up some snow. "Let me see that." I rubbed the snow on her arm. It washed away the dried blood, leaving the fresh, deep cuts in her arm exposed. The wounds made me sick to my stomach. "Don't ever do that again."

"Will you forgive me?"

"Yes. Now get back inside."

"Will you kiss me?"

"Yes."

She leaned forward and I met her halfway, pressing my lips against hers. We kissed intensely. Finally I pulled away. "We'll make plans after school. No one's going to find you."

"Okay. Whatever you say."

She got on her knees to go back inside. "I love you."

"I love you too," I said.

I walked back to the house. My mother was standing inside the door holding a bottle of maple syrup. She looked at me with a peculiar expression. "Were you talking to someone out there?"

I walked past her. "No."

CHAPTER
Twenty-nine

On the first day of Christmas my true love gave to me . . . a runaway in a clubhouse.

✵ GRACE'S DIARY ✵

School was a waste. I don't know why they bother to have half-days except to meet some bone-headed legislative requirement created by old fogies who haven't been to junior high for so long that they've forgotten what a wedgie feels like.

In English we did a crossword puzzle with Christmas themes and in math we used a Pascal triangle to determine the exact number of items accumulated in "The Twelve Days of Christmas." (The answer is three hundred sixty-four, sadly the only thing I remember from junior high math.) I did get one thing out of it. After class was dismissed, I asked my art teacher, Miss Tioné, about van Gogh. "Is it true he cut his ear off?"

"Yes."

"Why did he do that?"

"Well, there are a lot of different theories. Some people think he was drunk. Some say he did it to give to his beloved. Some even think another artist did it."

I looked down. "Oh."

"Why do you ask?"

"I just heard that sometimes people might hurt themselves when they feel bad."

The room was vacant except for the two of us, and she sat down at the desk next to me. "A few years back I had a student who had cuts on her arm. The first time I asked her about it she said she had a mean cat. But after a few weeks I knew she was doing it to herself. I asked her why. She told me that it was her way of dealing with strong feelings."

"Strong feelings?"

"Anger. Fear. Sorrow. Rejection."

"That makes sense," I said. "Thank you."

I noticed her glancing down at my arms.

"Eric, is there something you'd like to talk about?"

I looked at her and we both knew there was. "No, ma'am. But thank you."

She smiled sympathetically. "You're welcome. Have a nice Christmas."

"Thanks." I smiled and walked out of the room.

✵

After school I went straight to the Queen. Halfway through the night I raided the first-aid kit. I stole a bottle of iodine and a roll of white medical tape and gauze. When I got home I took everything to the clubhouse. I laid out the tape, then opened the bottle.

"Put your arm out," I said to Grace.

She was embarrassed to show me the cuts again, but she obeyed. The cuts—there were six in all—were dark and scabbed, each about three to four inches in length. I poured the entire bottle of antiseptic on her arm. There was alcohol in it and I thought she might cry out in pain but she just grimaced. Grace was pretty tough. The iodine stained her forearm a yellowish brown. I wrapped the gauze around her arm and taped it on. We didn't talk about why she had cut herself. I think that would have been more painful than the iodine.

When I finished she asked, "What day is it?"

"Tuesday."

"I mean the date."

"December eighteenth."

"It's just a week before Christmas." She frowned. "It doesn't feel like Christmas. Except for the snow."

"That's because you don't have any decorations." I thought about it. "I know, we can decorate the clubhouse. There are some Christmas lights in the garage. And I know where there's a perfect tree. It's way in back. No one will miss it."

"I've always wanted to cut down a real Christmas tree," Grace said.

"It's far enough back that no one will see you. We can do it tomorrow."

She pressed down the gauze, then looked up into my eyes. "I can't wait."

CHAPTER
Thirty

I feel so much happier now that we've decorated the clubhouse for Christmas. There is something healing about the season.

✦ GRACE'S DIARY ✦

WEDNESDAY, DEC. 19

As soon as I got home from school, Joel and I foraged through the garage for Christmas decorations. We found two boxes containing three long strings of tinsel garland, some red frosted glass balls, painted pine cones, a star for the tree, a wreath, and three strands of Christmas lights, which we thought we'd probably need to get just one to work. Back then if one bulb was bad the whole strand wouldn't light.

We also brought out a sled and about ten feet of rope to carry back our tree. We couldn't find the handsaw until Joel remembered that we'd left it in the chicken coop.

We took everything to the clubhouse. Grace squealed with delight when she saw what we'd found. We put everything inside, then the three of us started our trek to the back of our property. No one had been out back since the first snowfall so the snow was undisturbed and high, coming up to our thighs in places. We were all winded by the time we reached the tree. It looked shorter than I remembered since half of it was now buried beneath the snow.

"It's perfect," Grace said. "I know just where to put it."

It took the three of us a half hour to saw through the trunk. I could have done it faster myself but everyone wanted a turn. I finally finished it up. With the final cut I shouted, "Timber," which was more dramatic than the actual fall. We tied the tree on the sleigh and the three of us lugged it back to the clubhouse.

Our first attempts to get the tree inside failed. I hadn't considered the problem of getting a four-foot-wide tree through a three-foot door. We considered pounding out one of the walls, then nailing it back in—a task that would have taken us several hours. Then Grace suggested that we just flip the tree around and take it in trunk first, allowing the branches to naturally fold up. It worked.

We had no tree stand so we just leaned it in the corner in the bucket Grace had been using as an ice box.

Grace turned the radio on and cycled through stations until she found one playing Christmas music. Then we set about decorating the place. Bing Crosby's "White Christmas" filled the small room as we encircled the tree with the silver tinsel, then hung the ornaments.

Grace picked up the wreath. "I know where this is going," she said. She hung it right over Betty, which was the name she'd given the Vargas girl on our pinup poster.

To our surprise one of the strands of lights actually worked. "It's a Christmas miracle," Grace said.

I could never tell if she was joking.

CHAPTER
Thirty-one

**Is it better to be lonely or afraid?
I should know by now but I don't.**

✶ GRACE'S DIARY ✶

MONDAY, DEC. 24

That year Christmas Eve fell on a Monday. The Queen was closed. Not because Mr. Dick wanted us to be with our families but because experience had taught him that he'd lose money that day if he stayed open.

I spent the morning Christmas shopping. I followed my mother's suggestion and got Joel a new baseball and some baseball cards. I bought my mother some lilac-scented perfume and a pretty jewelry box and my father some of his favorite delicacies: a tin of sardines, a summer sausage, and a jar of herring in sour cream.

I had been working on a surprise for Grace for nearly three weeks. I wished that I could spend Christmas Eve with her but I knew it wasn't possible; we always went caroling as a family. I was more anxious about pulling off Christmas Day anyway.

Every Christmas Day our parents led us on an excruciating marathon of visits. It didn't really even matter who we visited. We'd go to old folks homes, homes of old friends, and just about anyone who claimed to be a relative. Now that we were in Utah we had a plethora of aunts and uncles to choose from. For my surprise to work, my family would have to go without me. I had a plan to make that happen.

✦

I came home and hid all my presents in the garage. Joel had gone shopping with my mom and dad. I went out back, knocked once on the clubhouse, then crawled inside. I had caught Grace off guard. She was crying.

"What's wrong?"

She wiped her eyes with the back of her hand. "Nothing."

I sat down next to her. "It's got to be something. You can tell me."

"I'm just emotional. Being pregnant . . ." She didn't finish but burst into tears. I put my arms around her.

"What is it?"

She suddenly sobbed out, "I miss my mom."

I pulled her closer. "I'm sorry."

"I . . . I . . ." She kept sobbing. ". . . I don't understand why she chose him over me."

"I'm so sorry," I said again. I didn't understand either. I just let her cry. When she began to settle down a little I said, "Tell me something."

"What?"

"What was Christmas in Hawaii like?"

She sniffed. "Well, it's different."

"In what way."

"Santa wears a swimsuit."

"That's not a pretty image."

She wiped her eyes. "And he comes on a surfboard. He wears a red Aloha shirt."

"That's groovy. What else?"

"Since they don't have chimneys, he leaves the gifts at the door."

Now I wiped her cheeks. "You need to

teach me how to say 'Merry Christmas' in Hawaiian."

"Mele Kalikimaka."

I tried. "Mel . . . vin Kawa . . . something."

"It's not that hard. Say what I say. Mele."

"Mele."

"Ka."

"Ka."

"Liki."

"Liki."

"Maka."

"Maka."

"Now all together. *Mele Kalikimaka.*"

"Mele . . . what you said."

She laughed. I was happy to hear it. "I know what you're doing," she said.

"You do?"

"Yes. And it's working."

"Good."

"I love you," she said.

I kissed her forehead. "I wish I could spend tonight with you."

"Me too. But I'll be okay."

"You're sure?"

"Yes."

"Promise me that you'll only think of

good things. I have a big surprise for you tomorrow. So promise."

"I promise."

"You'll be glad."

Then we kissed until I heard my family return.

CHAPTER

Thirty-two

There was once a place in Hawaii where women went to have babies. There were large stones that served as delivery tables, and the babies were delivered by the high chieftesses of Oahu. I would like to have gone there.

✦ GRACE'S DIARY ✦

TUESDAY, DEC. 25

Joel was always the first to wake on Christmas morning, though usually at some inhuman hour like four A.M. This led to the instigation of the "sunrise rule," which basically meant no waking our parents before there was discernible sunlight. It was overcast that morning so Joel got away with fudging it a little.

In our home, Christmas morning was governed by iron-clad tradition. Every year we started Christmas by gathering in my parents' bedroom to read the second chapter of Luke. I don't know how my mother remembered whose turn it was each year, or even if she really did, but she always seemed to know.

That morning it was my turn to read. In years past, fueled by the anticipation of Christmas surprises, I read as fast as humanly possible until my mother would tell me to slow down enough to be understood, or at least to auctioneer speed. This morning I was perfectly articulate. Partially because I was growing up and partially because, for the first time in my life, the words actually meant something to me.

And it came to pass in those days, that there went out a decree from Caesar Augustus, that all the world should be taxed . . .

As I thoughtfully read the words Joel looked crazed with anticipation. My father looked just as eager for me to finish but only because he wanted to go back to bed. Only my mother was smiling.

. . . And Joseph also went up from Galilee . . . unto the city of David . . . to be

taxed with Mary his espoused wife, being great with child. And so it was, that, while they were there, the days were accomplished that she should be delivered. And she brought forth her firstborn son, and wrapped him in swaddling clothes, and laid him in a manger: because there was no room for them in the inn.

I suppose that it meant more to me now that I understood a little of what Mary was going through. Grace was with child, and I took her in. The clubhouse was like a stable or at least not a whole lot nicer.

". . . Glory to God in the highest, and on earth peace, good will toward men."

After I read the scripture, my mother led us in a family prayer, then my dad got out his windup Brownie movie camera and went out into the living room to wait for us, shouting instructions like a Hollywood movie director.

Not surprisingly, there weren't a lot of presents that year and my parents had strategically spaced them to make it look

like more. I noticed that except for the in-
significant gifts that Joel and I had bought
for them, they hadn't bought gifts for each
other.

Joel got a new baseball mitt and bat,
which was all he really wanted, a navy
blue sweater and gray pants, and the ball
and baseball cards I had bought him.

I got a green argyle sweater and a pair
of brown corduroy pants, two board games,
Life and Mouse Trap, and a book about
frontier men. Joel got me a large box of
Swedish Fish.

After the last present was opened my
mom and dad went back to bed while Joel
and I played with our new treasures. About
an hour later, my mom got up to make
breakfast. I was setting up the Mouse Trap
game in the living room when my mother
came in and sat by me.

"I'm sorry there wasn't much this year,"
she said.

"I got plenty," I said, trying to balance
the game's small plastic teeter-totter. "Besides, that's not what Christmas is about."

My mother said nothing and I looked
up to see she was looking at me, pride

evident in her eyes. "Eric, I don't know everything that's happening in your life right now. But I know this has been a hard year for you; losing our home, coming to a new school, and leaving all your friends behind. But you've grown up so much. I'm so proud of you. Maybe coming to Utah wasn't such a bad thing."

I smiled. "Maybe not."

She smiled back at me. "Come on, let's have some breakfast."

✦

Mom always made special breakfasts on Christmas: cranberry corn muffins from scratch, hash brown potatoes with cheddar cheese, fried eggs, and sausage links. We looked forward to the Christmas breakfast table almost as much as the tree.

After breakfast we all helped my mother clean up. Joel and I put on our new sweaters and slacks while my parents dressed in their Sunday best.

Then I went into the bathroom and put a washcloth under hot water and held it to my forehead until it was hot. I dried my face with a towel and walked to my parents' room.

"Mom."

She was rubbing her hands with Jergens lotion. "Yes, dear?"

"I don't feel well. I think I have a fever."

She turned and looked at me. "You do look a little flushed." She put her cheek against my forehead. "You're warm."

"Would you mind too much if I just stayed home and went to bed?"

She frowned. "Maybe we should stay home with you."

I hadn't anticipated that response. "Mom, I'm almost fifteen."

"I know. But it's Christmas. I just want us to be together."

"I don't want to ruin your plans. I'll be okay."

She ran her fingers through my hair. "Okay. Why don't you go lie down and I'll get you some aspirin."

I went to my bed. She came in a few minutes later with a glass of water and two aspirin. "Here you are."

"Thank you." I took the pills and handed the glass back to my mother.

"We're going to be going soon. Do you need anything?"

"No. Thank you."

"If you need anything you can reach us at Aunt Estelle's or Aunt Gail's a little later. We won't be home until after dark."

"Okay," I said. "Have a good time."

"You get feeling better." She kissed my forehead. "Hmm. You already feel cooler."

"Must be good aspirin."

She grinned. "Merry Christmas."

"Merry Christmas, Mom."

Five minutes later Joel walked into the room. He was angry. "You faker! Now I have to go alone."

"Sorry."

"No you're not. You just want to be with *her.*"

"We have special plans."

"But what about me?" His face screwed up like he was going to cry, then he stomped out.

As soon as the Bee pulled out of the driveway I got out of bed and went to my parents' bedroom. I got in my mother's drawer and took out one of her silk scarves. Then I set about getting ready for my surprise. It was more than an hour later when I went to get Grace.

CHAPTER

Thirty-three

Eric has given me the greatest Christmas of my life and the greatest gift. I gave him truth, and he still loved me.

✨ GRACE'S DIARY ✨

"Just a minute," Grace said as she came out. She held two small packages in her hand.

"What's that?"

"I have surprises too."

When we got to the house I pulled the scarf from my pocket. "Before you go in, I need to blindfold you."

"How exciting."

I rolled the scarf up and tied it around her eyes, then took her by the arm, opened the door, and led her through the kitchen into our dining room. I took the things she carried and set them on the table.

"Just a minute. Don't go anywhere."

"It smells like coconuts," she said. "What are you doing?"

I turned on the living room stereo. The bright strum of a ukulele filled the room.

"Hawaiian music," she said.

While she stood there, blindfolded, I kissed her. I didn't think her smile could have grown larger but it did. "That's a nice surprise."

"That wasn't my surprise. Just an opportunity." I untied the scarf.

She rubbed her eyes then looked around the room.

"*Mele Kalikimaka*," I said. "Welcome to Hawaii." I had clipped pictures of Hawaii (as well as a few places that I thought looked like Hawaii, like Fiji and Formosa) from my mom's *National Geographic* magazines and hung them on the walls of the kitchen. I had decorated the table with a thatched bamboo runner, and on the table there were two candles placed in coconut shells.

"Candles," Grace said.

"Well, they were supposed to be tiki torches, but I couldn't find any of those."

She laughed. "Good thing. Try explaining to your parents how you burned down their house holding a luau for a runaway girl."

I smiled. "Before we eat we need to dress the part." I lifted a small box from the table. "For you."

"Really?" She lifted the lid and her face lit up. She pulled out the cloth inside.

"It's a Hawaiian muumuu."

She let it unfold. "Oh, it's beautiful. Should I put it on now?"

I nodded. "You remember where the bathroom is?"

"I do," she said.

"But first." I handed her another box. She excitedly lifted the lid. Inside there was a bright red flower. "That's for your hair."

She was positively beaming. "I'll be right back."

She walked down the hall to the bathroom. When the door shut, I went to my room and put on a bright red Hawaian shirt and a plastic lei. Then I went back to the dining room. When she walked in, I just stared. She had never looked more beautiful. Her eyes sparkled, and the soft fabric of her dress hung gracefully on her body. She was glowing. I was tongue-tied.

"Look at you," she said. "You look so cute."

"I'd much rather look at you."

"Thank you," she said coyly. "I like the flower. I thought it was plastic, but it's real."

"I know. They look fake. It's called an anthurium. But I'm sure you already knew that."

She just smiled at me.

"I have a lei for you too, but it really is plastic." As I draped the lei around her neck, she kissed me. Then she whispered, "*Mele Kalikimaka* to you too."

I pulled out her chair, and she sat down.

"For dinner I made us a Hawaiian luau feast. At least the best I could do in Utah. I'll be back."

I went to the kitchen and brought back our first course: a bowl of pineapple chunks in heavy syrup and two virgin piña coladas with little paper umbrellas.

She clapped with delight.

"There's a Polynesian woman at Heller's. She told me what to make."

Over the next hour I brought out ham and white rice, rice noodles, and yams.

As we were finishing the last course, she said, "I can't believe you really made all this."

"Pretty much. Except what's next."

"What's next?"

"Glad you asked." I went to the kitchen and brought back a pineapple upside-down cake. "Dessert."

I set it down at the table and cut two pieces, serving hers first. Then I sat down, watching her expectantly. She took a small bite.

"How is it?"

"It's delicious."

"Do they eat that in Hawaii?"

She picked up a piece of the cake and held it to my mouth. "You try it."

I took a bite. "That is good."

"Told you."

For a moment we just looked at each other. The earlier excitement had evolved into pleasant peace. Then I said, "Remember that night when I asked you how you really know when you were in love?"

"Yes."

"I understand."

Grace's eyes began to well up with tears. She came over and sat on my lap; laying her head on my shoulder. She began to cry softly. I gently rubbed her back. "It's okay."

"This is the best day of my life. You're the answer to all my prayers."

She leaned back from me and wiped her eyes.

"Oh, our candles are going out," I said. The smoke from a dying candle snaked up toward the ceiling.

She turned back and looked at the remaining candle. "Before it goes out, what do you want to know more than anything?"

I didn't answer her for a long time. Then my smile vanished.

When she saw me frown, her smile disappeared as well. "What is it?"

I looked down, afraid to say what I was thinking. "Nothing."

"No, what is it?"

I took a deep breath. "I want to know how this ends."

She breathed out slowly, then she turned and stared into the flame. It felt like forever before she spoke. "My stepfather is gone."

"Where?"

"Somewhere he can't hurt anyone ever again."

I waited for more but she didn't offer anything. "Where are you?"

She didn't answer.

"Do you see Hawaii?"

She stared into the flame and I saw a trace of sadness in her eyes. Suddenly she looked back at me, as if the flame had released her. "I see Hawaii all around me," she said. She kissed me. Then she said, "Let's dance." She took my hands and pulled me up.

The song playing was slow, a Hawaiian lullaby. She draped her arms around my neck, resting her head on my shoulder. I put my arms around her waist, savoring the warmth of her body next to mine. We gently rocked back and forth. It was the greatest moment of my life. Suddenly she leaned back. "I haven't been completely honest with you."

"About what?"

"Promise me you won't be angry."

"You couldn't say anything that would make me angry."

"Okay." She closed her eyes tightly then

touched her forehead to mine. "I've never been to Hawaii."

"What?"

"I'm from Cheyenne, Wyoming."

We stopped swaying. "Wyoming?"

"Hawaii was just someplace I've always wanted to be, the way some people think of heaven. After Stan . . ." She paused with the hurt that name carried. "It was a place I would go in my mind when he was . . . hurting me." She looked at me. "Hawaii was my dream. And you gave it to me." A tear fell down her cheek.

"It's okay," I said. "I don't care where you're from. I'm just glad you're here." I tried to pull her back into me but she stopped me.

"There's something else I have to tell you." She looked down for a moment, then back into my eyes. She brushed a strand of hair from her face. "I called my aunt."

"The one who hates you?"

"She doesn't hate me. She was really nice. I found out what really happened between her and my mom. Before my mother got married, she told her that she didn't like Stan and that she shouldn't marry him.

My mother got really upset and told her she never wanted to talk to her again. Then my mother told Stan and he called and screamed at her and told her if he ever saw her or if she called the house she'd regret it. She was actually worried about us. Especially me. When I told her that I'd run away she said she wasn't surprised. She asked me to come live with her."

"In Denver?"

Grace nodded.

"Did you tell her *everything?*"

"I told her about the baby."

"What did she say?"

"She didn't ask who the father was. I wasn't ready to tell her yet. But she said it was good that I called and that she'd help me. She wanted me to come right away."

"When was this?"

"Last Friday. I told her that I couldn't leave before Christmas."

"Why not?"

She looked at me, puzzled that I didn't know. "Because of you. I don't want to leave you."

Now my eyes filled with tears.

It was a few moments before I could

speak. "This is good news, right?" I said, trying to sound happy.

"Yes. It is."

"When are you leaving?"

"Friday."

I looked down. She suddenly smiled. "You should come with me."

"I can't."

"I know it's impossible. I just . . ." She paused. ". . . I can't imagine being without you. You're the best friend I've ever had. You're the best thing that's ever happened to me."

She fell back into me and I pulled my arms tightly around her. We gently swayed through three or four more songs until the vinyl record began skipping. I went and put the needle back at the beginning of the record. When I returned she was sitting down.

"I have presents for you too."

I sat down. She handed me two gifts. One was a small box wrapped in shiny red paper. The other was a piece of parchment rolled up in a scroll and tied with a yellow ribbon. "They're not as good as yours."

"I'll be the judge of that." I unwrapped the first package; it was a small blue velvet jeweler's box. I opened the lid; inside was an ornate silver locket.

"It's not for you to wear," she said. "It's for you to hold."

I looked at her, my heart feeling things I'd never felt before. "Thank you."

"Open it."

I unclasped the locket. On one side, beneath a small glass pane, was a picture of Grace. On the other side, also beneath glass, was a strand of her hair.

"I thought this way, no matter what happens, you could always have some of me near you."

No matter what happens. Something about the way she said this frightened me. She handed me the scrolled up parchment.

I gently unrolled it. It was a poem written in her graceful handwriting. I read it aloud.

I WOULD
By Grace Webb

If only I could shine in your life as you have in mine. I would.
If only I could love you as deeply as you have loved me. I would.

**If only I could heal your heart as you have
healed mine. I would.**

**If only I could lead you to God as you
have led me. I would.**

**If only I could give you the hope that
you've given me. I would.**

**If only I could stay with you forever. I
would.**

We kissed and I held her until it was
dark outside. Then I called my Aunt Marge's
house and asked to speak to my mother.
She asked how I was feeling and if I had
made myself something to eat. She said
they would be home in about an hour.
Grace helped me clean up. After we finished we went back out to the clubhouse
and held each other and talked until we
heard the Bee pull into the driveway. I suppose that was one good thing about the
Bee; you could hear it coming a block
away. I went back inside and climbed in my
bed. My mother came in to check on me.

"Your eyes are red," she said.

"I know. But I'll be okay."

Joel didn't say anything to me. It was
just as well. Grace was leaving in two days.

I didn't know how to begin to think about my life without her.

It was the best and worst night of my entire life.

CHAPTER

Thirty-four

I have been preparing all day for my trip to Colorado. I know it's the right thing to do, but I can't stop crying. I'm going to miss him so much.

✴ GRACE'S DIARY ✴

THURSDAY, DEC. 27

Predictably work was boring, but it was not without some pleasure: Dean quit. I would have shouted with joy had decorum allowed; I did buy myself an Orange Crush to celebrate. I couldn't wait to tell Grace. At eleven o'clock sharp I locked the back door, hopped on my bike, and pedaled home.

As I rounded the corner at the top of my street I heard a strange noise, a loud chirp followed by a blast of static. It wasn't until I was two houses away from my home that

I discovered the source; there was a black and white patrol car parked in my driveway. I wanted to turn around, but I didn't; I didn't know what to do. As I rode to the garage to put my bike away I wondered if I should tell Grace.

Instead, I walked through the back door hoping the police were parked out front for any reason other than the one I feared. Maybe they'd found out I had played hooky from school.

"I'm home," I said as I entered. I headed straight for the darkened corridor that led to my bedroom.

"Eric," my mother called from the living room.

I stopped. My heart was pounding so hard I could hear it.

"Come here, please."

My father sat in his La-Z-Boy and my mother sat next to him in a chair she'd pulled in from the kitchen. Two police officers sat across from them on the couch. Everyone was looking at me.

One of the officers was young and tall with yellow hair, the other older, balding, rotund, and as short as my mother. Their guns and holsters looked remarkably out of place in our living room. My father looked angry and my mother just looked tense.

"Yes?" I tried to keep my voice from cracking.

The older officer spoke first. "Eric, I'm Officer Steele of the Salt Lake County Sheriff's Office and this is Officer Buttars. Do you know this young woman?" He lifted a copy of the poster of Grace I had seen at the Queen and a dozen other places.

My throat suddenly felt impossibly dry. I swallowed.

"Eric," my father prodded. "Answer them."

"Sure. Everyone does. She's the girl from my school."

"Do you know where she is?"

"No." I looked past them to a family portrait on the wall.

"We've been told by a witness that you've been seen with her," the young policeman said.

"Who told you that?" I asked.

"That's not important."

How was that not important? "I don't know where she is," I said.

"Have you seen her in the last week?" he asked.

I shouted, "I said I don't know!"

My explosion caught everyone off guard including myself. No one spoke for a moment. Then Officer Steele said, "Young man, this is a very serious matter. Taking someone against their will is kidnapping. It's a crime that carries a long prison term."

"I didn't kidnap her."

"Eric," my mother said. "Where is Madeline?"

I glanced between them, feeling as transparent as Scotch tape. I was bad at this. I could tell that they knew that I knew. Dread grew heavy in my stomach like a cannon ball. I wanted to go to bed. "Can I go now?"

"Eric," my mother repeated firmly, "do you know where Madeline Webb is?"

After a few minutes I took a deep breath then slowly exhaled. "I can't tell you."

"Can't, or won't?" the young policeman said.

My mother said gently, "Eric. If you know where she is you need to tell us."

"I can't."

Officer Steele started, "Young man, if—"

My mother interrupted him. Her voice was still calm. "Why can't you tell us, Eric?"

"They'll hurt her."

"Who will?" she asked.

"I can't tell you."

Officer Steele looked at his partner, then at me. "Son, we've met with Madeline's parents many times. I'm sure they would never let anyone hurt her. They are as concerned as any loving parents would be for their daughter." He turned to my parents. "Her poor parents . . ."

I glared at him. *Was he really that stupid?*

The young policeman joined in. "Son, you're harboring a fugitive. Do the right thing here and tell us where she is."

I looked at the floor for what seemed like ten minutes. I could hear the clock in the kitchen ticking.

"Eric!" my father shouted. I jumped. But still I said nothing. I don't know how long we were there. I felt like a fugitive myself held up in a house surrounded by the police. *Give yourself up. There's no way out of this, Eric.* My brain ached.

"Tell us where she is, son," Officer Steele said gently.

I took a deep breath then slowly let it out. "She's in the clubhouse."

Officer Steele turned to my mother. "What did he say?"

My mother looked at me sympathetically. "The boys built a clubhouse in the backyard," she said.

Both the policemen were immediately on their feet, no doubt excited at the prospect of being the heroes who found the missing girl and brought her home. To me they were the enemy, as stupid as all adults seemed to be those days. And my parents had been complicit, abetting the enemy.

"Take us to her," the young policeman said.

In times of high stress I've found that my mind fixates on the trivial. I suppose it's a defense mechanism. Suddenly all I could see was the guy's feet. They seemed impossibly large, like frogman flippers. I just stared at them until my thoughts were broken by the sound of my dad clearing his throat. I looked up at him. He had the gray look of disappointment in his eyes but I honestly didn't care. His disappointment in me couldn't be a fraction of mine in him. For the first time in my life I measured my thoughts against his with equal value. No, *more* so. My actions came from love and duty. His came from ignorance. I suppose it was at that moment I became a man.

Officer Steele walked to my side, grabbing the back of my arm. "Let's go."

"I need my boots." I walked to the kitchen to get them. I considered making a run to the clubhouse to tell Grace, but Officer Steele followed me back. I picked them up and returned to the front room. I sat on the floor slowly putting them on, but I could only delay so much.

We went out the front door, then turned back down the driveway, trudging through the snow. I felt as if my feet were carrying me against my will.

Even the moon betrayed Grace that night. It was bright and naked, only slightly blistered by thin, black clouds. It turned the snow-packed ground luminescent. I felt like Judas leading the Roman soldiers to Gethsemane. *At least Jesus knew he'd been betrayed.* It sickened me that Grace had no idea what was coming.

Then I grabbed on to a thought as frantically as a drowning man grabbing a life preserver. Maybe *she did know* we were coming. Maybe she had, like me, heard the police radio. Of course she had. I heard it all the way down the street. *Or maybe she had seen it all in the candle.*

We stopped a few yards in front of the clubhouse.

"This it?" Officer Steele asked.

I didn't answer. It was a stupid question.

He walked over as if inspecting Joel's and my work. He pointed at the door. "Is this the only door?"

My father, leaning on his crutches, turned to me. I nodded.

The officer put his hand on the front of our structure and leaned in close. He knocked sharply on the door and said, "Madeline, it's Officer Steele of the Salt Lake County Sheriff's Office."

We all stood there staring at the door. There was no sound.

"Madeline, we're not going to hurt you. We're here to make sure you're all right."

Nothing stirred. The policeman got down on one knee and pushed the door open. It was as dark as a cave inside.

"She probably left," I said angrily. "She probably knew you were coming."

He looked at me. "How would she know that?"

"She just knows things."

"Get me a flashlight," Officer Steele said to his partner.

Officer Buttars left, the sound of his flipper feet clomping through the thick snow as loud as if he were stomping bags of potato chips. *With those paddles he should have just walked on top of the snow.* I could feel my mother's gaze on me but I didn't look at her. I didn't look at anyone. My eyes were fixed on the little door, fearing that Grace would suddenly appear. As the minutes passed, I started to feel some hope that maybe she had run away.

It seemed an eternity before the younger policeman returned carrying a long silver flashlight that no doubt doubled as a truncheon. He handed it to Officer Steele who pushed open the door, panning inside with the light until he fixed on one point. Then he looked back at his partner and nodded.

My heart stopped. I could only imagine

Grace curled up in the corner, shaking and frightened. I wanted to run and tackle him and yell for Grace to run. But I didn't. I just stood as frozen by guilt as fear.

"Are you Madeline Webb?" he asked. I couldn't hear Grace say anything but from the officer's body language I knew that Grace had responded. "Let's go, Madeline, it's time to go home."

Only then did I hear Grace's soft voice. I don't know what she said, but the sound of it sent chills through me. More than anything I wanted to run. The Bible talks of a sinner feeling shame so great that he wishes for a mountain to fall on him. At that moment I wished for that mountain. Or one of Khrushchev's missiles.

The officer stood back from the door. And then I saw her, her hands in the snow, her head crowning at the entrance. She pushed herself up. She had nothing with her but her coat.

"Are you okay?" Officer Steele asked. She nodded slightly. She didn't look at me. I didn't know what I would do if she did. "Have you been kept here against your will?"

"No."

"You're not going to try to run away from us are you?" the young policeman asked. "We don't want to handcuff you."

"Don't touch her," I said.

Only then did she look at me, and I saw in her eyes that she was no longer mine to protect. I had lost the right to speak for her.

Officer Steele put his hand on her shoulder and gently pushed her forward. She walked ahead of us, flanked by the policemen. My parents walked behind me. When we got to the driveway the young officer opened the back door of the patrol car and Grace got in. She didn't even look at me.

My parents and I stood there at the edge of our driveway. I had never felt more alone in my life. I felt estranged even from myself, brimming with self-hate. In the darkness beneath the trees the policemen were no longer people, like Grace, they had turned to shadow, like shades in the land of the dead, on the banks of the river Styx.

The patrol car's engine roared to life, then its headlights blinked on, momentarily blinding us. The car pulled out of our driveway, crunching and spinning on the icy gravel.

I just stood there. After all we'd been through, just like that she was gone.

My dad said, "Let's go to bed, Eric. We'll talk in the morning."

Then my mom said, "You did the right thing."

At that moment I saw that my parents were as capable of evil and stupidity as anyone who has ever walked this planet. They were as capable of evil as me.

I walked into the house without a word. I kicked the boots from my feet and trudged off to my bedroom. The room was dark; as usual Joel had gone to bed hours earlier. I took off my pants, then climbed under the covers. The prospect of sleeping seemed ridiculous. I felt sick to my stomach. I wished I could vomit the whole night away.

I suddenly became aware of Joel's breathing. I don't know why but the sound filled me with rage. After a minute Joel said softly, "Did they take her?"

For a moment I couldn't speak. All the rage and fear and anger twisted my mind into a horrible, tight knot. Then I exploded, throwing back my covers and glaring wild-eyed at my little brother.

"You told them! You said you'd never tell and you did!"

Even in the dark I could see his eyes, wide and frightened. "No I didn't. I didn't tell *anyone*."

"You're a liar!" I hissed. "And she's going to get hurt. Do you *know* what her father will do to her? And it's all your fault."

His voice cracked. "I didn't tell anyone, Eric. I promise."

Deep in my heart I knew he was telling the truth, but my heart wasn't in control. "I'm never going to talk to you again. Never. I hate you."

My words fell off into silence. I could hear Joel softly crying beneath his covers, whimpering over and over, "I didn't do it."

I had committed my second act of treason of the night.

CHAPTER

Thirty-five

I had a dream that the whole world turned to glass. Those who had much to hide were very afraid.

✦ GRACE'S DIARY ✦

FRIDAY, DEC. 28

I don't know what time it was when I woke the next morning, but no one was home. I looked over to Joel's bed. It was made. I just lay back in my bed looking at the ceiling, following its cracks with my eyes, trying to distract myself from what I felt. My heart ached in a way I had never felt before. Grace was gone. I had cut off my brother and I had unmasked my parents as the sinners they were. I had never felt so alone in all my life. It was the first time in my life that I truly wanted to die.

What seemed unbelievable to me was that Grace was still out there. Was there a chance that she would be okay? Maybe the police were telling the truth and her parents really wanted to take care of her. Right, and Kennedy and Khrushchev were playing croquet together.

Even if she weren't hurt, I had betrayed her. It was no use trying to believe that everything was okay. It wasn't. And it never would be again.

CHAPTER

Thirty-six

The greatest pain of most trials comes from the uncertainty. To free ourselves of pain we must first submit to it.

✦ GRACE'S DIARY ✦

WEDNESDAY, JAN. 2

Wednesday morning came like the flu. My thoughts about seeing Grace at school couldn't have been more divided. Half of me couldn't wait to see her. The other half was terrified. I wondered what she would do.

I looked for Grace in the halls. At lunch I walked around the lunchroom, then I walked to her locker. I didn't see her. At least, I thought, I would see her in Spanish.

I got to class early, then I waited outside the classroom until the bell rang. As I walked into the room I glanced toward her desk; it was empty. Then I sat down in my seat, glancing every few seconds at the door. Only after the tardy bell rang did I believe that she wasn't coming. It made sense that she wasn't there. After being away from home that long, her parents probably wouldn't let her out of their sight. Then again, they might have discovered that she was pregnant. In those days unwed mothers sometimes just disappeared, whisked off to other cities so as not to shame their family. Part of me was relieved that she hadn't come, but it was equally matched by disappointment. I missed her. Even her hating me wouldn't change that.

I don't remember hearing anything in class but my mental absence seemed to pass unnoticed. The final bell rang and, like everyone else, I began gathering my books when Mrs. Waller tapped a ruler against the blackboard to get our attention.

"Class, please stay in your seats for just a moment. I need your attention."

The class quieted.

"As you know, one of our classmates,

Madeline Webb, had been missing. We heard today that she passed away over the holiday. For those of you who were close to her, I'm very sorry."

The class rose around me and flowed past my desk. I sat there unable to move. Suddenly the tears started to come. I covered my eyes and put my head down on my desk and began to shake. I don't know how long I sat that way before I felt a hand on my shoulder.

"I'm so sorry, Eric." Mrs. Waller stood next to my desk.

When I could speak I asked, "What happened?"

She hesitated. "I can't tell you."

I looked at her, my eyes wet, dark and direct. "It was her stepfather, wasn't it?"

She didn't answer me.

"I'm going to kill him."

"He's in jail, Eric."

I began to sob. She stood there with her hand on my back with no idea what to say.

✦

I purposely missed the bus. I walked home, glad for the pain and cold. I now understood why Grace had cut herself. I wanted to cut out my heart.

For the first time since I started school in Utah, my mother was home when I got there. From the way she looked at me I knew that she knew about Grace. I walked past her without speaking. I went to my bedroom and slammed the door. I hated her for knowing what had happened.

She followed me and stood outside my door. "Eric."

I wasn't about to give her the satisfaction of needing her sympathy. "What do you want?"

"Did you hear . . ."

"Did I hear what?"

She paused. "Did you hear about Madeline?"

"What about it?" I said.

"I'm sorry," she said and walked away.

CHAPTER

Thirty-seven

To hate is to feel strong and to be weak.

✦ GRACE'S DIARY ✦

For the next two days I didn't speak to anyone in the house. I could see the pain my silence caused them and it made me glad. Whether it was misery looking for company or the pursuit of vengeance I don't know. I wasn't really that introspective. It was probably a little of both.

Every time my mother tried to speak to me I walked away from her. Disrespect wasn't tolerated in our home but this time neither of my parents challenged me. Maybe they realized what they'd done and felt the guilt I thought they deserved. Or maybe they instinctively sensed just how close I was to the edge. I *was* close. There was something new inside me. Something that felt strong. It had no heart, no reason, and, most exquisitely, no fear. It was hate. It welcomed a confrontation. It hoped for one.

I had decided to run away. I had already packed what I needed and decided to leave the night of Grace's funeral. I had a pretty good idea of what running away would entail. I had taken care of a runaway. I could take care of myself. Even if I couldn't it didn't matter. If I had learned one thing from all this it was clarity. I knew who the enemy was. And I would do anything to punish them, including hurt myself.

✦

Friday night my mother came to my room. I was alone, as Joel had slept with my parents every night since I'd turned on him. The light was off and I was in my bed, though a thousand hours from sleeping. She knocked once, then stepped inside, staying close to the doorway.

"Eric, can we talk?" she asked softly.

I didn't answer but rolled to my side. I could hear her swallow. She just stood there, a shadow, wondering what to do.

Finally she said, "Madeline's funeral is tomorrow at noon. We'll all be going. I hope you come with us."

I didn't answer. She sighed. "Good night."

She shut the door.

I shouted after her. "Her name isn't Madeline!"

✦

The next day I slept in until eleven, showered, and got dressed. I stayed in my room until it was time to go, then I walked out and got in the van before anyone else did. No one spoke to me.

The funeral was held at a small church near her home. Before the service they had an open casket viewing. I climbed out of the van and walked inside, apart from my parents. I followed the signs to a small room.

I wasn't prepared for what I saw, but I don't know how I could have been. There was Grace in a wooden casket. The inside was lined with pink satin. She looked like she was sleeping. My heart felt as if it were being torn apart.

A short, stout woman with black hair stood next to the casket. She looked frail and her eyes were puffy. I knew who she was and I immediately hated her. I hated her for her weakness and her betrayal of her own daughter. *Now* she stood by her side. I wanted to shout at her. *Hypocrite! Why weren't you at her side when she needed you?*

My parents stood in line and walked up to the casket. Joel held my mother's hand. He was crying. My parents paid their condolences to Grace's mother, which only made me angrier. They deserved each other. A party of traitors.

I kept my distance, standing at the side of the room torn between my hate and unspeakable sorrow. I wanted to wake her and run away with her, but Grace wasn't there. Grace was life and spirit and there was none of that here. It was just a body in a box. Grace had gone someplace else. I wished I could have gone with her.

Sometime later the minister said they would be closing the casket and if anyone wanted to give the deceased their last regards now was the time. A few people walked to the casket and kissed Grace. Then her mother fell on her, crying, "My baby. My darling baby."

Everyone in the room watched, moved by the emotional outburst. Many of them started to cry as well. A man in a suit comforted her. I just stood there, watching the drama unfold like bad theater.

I didn't sit by my family for the service. I sat alone staring at the back of a pew while people who didn't really know anything about Grace talked about her as if they suddenly cared.

As we were leaving the funeral I felt a hand touch my shoulder. I turned around. It was Grace's mother.

"Are you Eric?"

I just glared at her.

"You're Eric. I know you are. I just wanted you to know that . . ." She began to cry. I stared at her, unwilling to offer sympathy. Her voice pitched. ". . . My baby wanted you. When the ambulance came for her, she asked for you. Your name was the last thing she said."

I just looked at her as she wiped her eyes with a crumpled tissue.

"Thank you for being there for her."

"If I was there for her we wouldn't be here," I said. I turned and walked away.

CHAPTER
Thirty-eight

To truly forgive is to accept our own part of each failure.

✦ GRACE'S DIARY ✦

God flooded Noah's world so why couldn't he have cleansed the earth again? I knew enough theology to remember that a baptism by water is followed by a baptism by fire. Fire seemed appropriate. That coward Khrushchev had missed his calling.

My parents, Joel, and I walked into the house without a word. I was done with my family. I had enough money to make it to Denver to see Grace's aunt. And then who knew. The truth is I didn't care where I went. I spent far less time thinking about where I was going than what I was leaving.

My mother followed me to my room. "Eric." She tried to put her arms around me but I pulled away.

"Stay away from me."

"Eric. You have to talk about this."

"I don't talk to murderers."

"Murderers?"

"You killed her. You and Dad and Joel and her pathetic, worthless mother and those stupid, idiotic policemen who just couldn't wait to be heroes. I told you they would hurt her and you made me tell them. You killed Grace. You all killed Grace. I hate you. I hate all of you. You should have died, not her."

My mother was stunned, but her gaze was still full of compassion. "No, Eric. We didn't kill her."

"You and the police and Joel . . . you all killed her."

"Eric, her stepfather killed her."

Then, I fell against the wall, sobbing uncontrollably. "No," I said. "I killed her. I told you where she was. She'd still be alive if it wasn't for me."

My mother put her hands on my shoulders and turned me toward her. Tears were running down her face. Her voice was strong but loving. "Eric, listen to me. We didn't kill her. You didn't kill her. A very bad very sick man killed her, not you. You tried to protect her. But you're only fourteen. It was too big for you. You did the best you could. You loved her and she loved you."

"She'll never forgive me," I said. "She shouldn't forgive me." My knees buckled and I fell to the ground.

My mother crouched down, holding me. "Eric, sometimes horrible, unspeakable things happen in life. What happened was wrong. But it's not your fault."

I looked at my mother, my face twisted in anguish. "I miss her so much, Mom, I want to die. I want to die."

My mother was crying as hard as I was. She stroked my forehead. "I know you loved her, sweetheart."

"I can't stand the pain. What do I do?"

She pulled my head in next to her cheek. "You just keep on living, Eric. And you hope."

"Hope for what?"

"For grace."

CHAPTER

Thirty-nine

**Though your sins be as scarlet,
they shall be as white as snow . . .**

✴ ISAIAH 1:18 ✴

It snowed Saturday night.

Outside my window the winter wind had rippled the snow like sand dunes, piling drifts in crusted peaks.

I put on my tennis shoes and climbed out my window onto the crystalline blanket. The snow slid up my pants and bit my legs.

For the first time since Grace left, I returned to the clubhouse. Our footprints from that night were gone, evidence covered over at a crime scene. Everything was white.

The clubhouse didn't look the same to me. It was the same feeling I had at the funeral service staring across the room at Grace's body. She was gone. The club-house was just a corpse.

I kicked at the snow by the door and pried it open.

I crawled in and turned on the light. There was frost on the walls and the Christmas tree was still there, the water in its bucket frozen hard. Grace's things were there, just as she had left them. On top of the sleeping bag was her yellow diary.

I held it for a moment before I opened it and began to read what she'd written. She had recorded all that she'd been through, the horror and the joy. My emotions rose and fell with each page. The happiness she felt that her mother had found some-one and her disappointment when she saw the real side of the man. She wrote of the first time Stan had gotten to her. And the day she realized she was pregnant.

I suppose the diary was a prayer of sorts, written only for God's eyes. On nearly every page she wrote of her hopes of finding someone to help her. Someone to love her. That is, up until the day she met me. As I read each page I realized what my role had been in her life and how much I meant to her. The last thing she wrote was this.

He is the only thing on this earth I believe in. Eric is my Hawaii.

I stared at those words. Then I closed the book and held it near my chest and I curled up in a fetal position. I had been there for a long time, when I heard something outside. I looked over to the door. Joel was there, looking at me. He was afraid of me, but he was there, just like he always had been.

"Hi," I said. I sat up, my back pressed against the wall.

He crawled the rest of the way in and sat down next to me, his knees touching mine. We sat without words, both of us looking down at our feet. "It's cold," he said.

I took a deep breath. "I'm sorry I got mad at you. I know it wasn't your fault."

"It's okay."

"No, it's not. You're my best friend."

Joel's eyes welled up. "I've missed you."

I put my arm around him. "I've missed you too, buddy."

"I really liked her," he said.

Then I began to cry. "I know. So did I."

The truest grace is not to forgive, but to have never found fault.

✨ GRACE'S DIARY ✨

✦ EPILOGUE ✦

Christmas tales have always been about redemption. I suppose that's what Christmas is all about. My whole life I have hoped for redemption. Redemption and grace. I don't deserve it, but I still hope.

My father fully recovered from the Guillain-Barré. By the next summer he was walking without crutches. We moved from that dump of a neighborhood and built a home in the Cottonwood area, a nice suburb of Holladay. Not long after, my aunts and uncles sold the old house to developers, who bulldozed it, along with the clubhouse, to put up low-rent apartment units. I was glad to know it was all gone.

Years passed. My father was diagnosed with testicular cancer. He died July 4th of 1976, the day America celebrated its Bicentennial. My mother is still alive. She resides in southern California in a townhouse about a mile from Joel. She never remarried.

Joel and I never spent a summer together like that again. By the next summer I was into cars and girls and all that comes with growing up. But Joel did all right for himself. Turns out he was better at baseball than any of us knew. He made the varsity baseball team his sophomore year of high school—the first time a sophomore had ever done that. He wore his letterman jacket and had a thousand friends and even more girlfriends. Unlike me, Joel managed to be cool.

He made All State in baseball his junior year and by his senior year word of his talent had spread wide enough that he was hounded by scouts from every major college. Joel returned to California, attending UCLA on a full-ride athletic scholarship. He played in the Pioneer Leagues for two years, then played second base for the Mets for another six before his knees gave out. He has a baseball card with his face on it. Imagine that, my little brother on a baseball card. Just like DiMaggio.

Today he has a beautiful wife, four children, two grandchildren, and a ten-thousand-square-foot house with a swimming pool surrounded by potted kumquat trees. He owns a Honda dealership in Simi Valley. We talk on the phone every Sunday night. I miss him.

Hard things, if they don't kill you, make you grow. Sometimes they even make you lose your fear. I never backed down again. A week after the funeral, one of the hoods bullied me. It took two teachers to pull me off of him. He and his friends never bothered me again.

I became a serious student with good enough grades to get accepted to Stanford Law School. After graduation I returned to Utah and at the age of twenty-nine I was made assistant prosecutor at the Utah Attorney General's Office. At thirty-four I was appointed the youngest prosecutor in the state's history. I have spent my life hunting down and prosecuting people like Grace's stepfather. I carry Grace's locket into every trial. I've earned a reputation as a fierce courtroom combatant who takes every case personally. What Grace saw in the candle was true of me as well. I am feared.

A reporter once asked me what drove me. I looked down for a moment, then softly replied, "Grace." She wrote it down but she didn't understand. I wouldn't have explained anyway.

I don't know what happened to Grace's mother; all I know is that she moved out of Utah. A part of me hopes she's in Hawaii. Grace would have liked that.

Stan is still alive, or he was the last time I checked. He got out of prison after seventeen years for "good behavior." I've seen him. I paid him a visit after his release to a halfway house. I needed to know for myself that he wasn't still a threat. I also wanted to let him know that I was, and that I was watching him. My visit wasn't necessary. He was a broken shell of a man; nothing but a shadow and a stain. I thought of the line from Isaiah: They that see thee shall narrowly look upon thee, and consider thee, saying, Is this the man that made the earth to tremble?

I don't know if he paid his debt—that's up to God to decide—but he took something beautiful from this earth. He took something that no one could ever give back.

*

Today I continue my crusade. I have testified about child abuse before state lawmakers more times than I can remember. I've lived to see child advocacy become a public concern. I am grateful that the world finally has the courage to open its eyes. My wife asks me when we can retire, but I tell her I'll die in the saddle. With my last breath I'll continue to fight for these children. I cannot save them all, but I can save some of them, and that's worth doing. There are other Graces out there.

*

When I was a ten-year-old boy sitting in a Methodist Sunday school, my teacher asked what we would do if we had been at Calvary. Would we deny Jesus like Peter had? Or would we carry Jesus' cross? As one who had read more than his fair share of comic books, I said I would take a machine gun and mow down all the Roman soldiers who were crucifying Jesus. My teacher nodded understandingly, then asked, "Then who would save us?"

I was never able to answer this. The whole thing seemed just a colossal miscarriage of justice, but then, I guess that's the point. But this has always been God's way, wringing good from evil. In some ways, this is true of Grace's life.

I loved Grace; time has only confirmed this to me. But life goes on and so must we. At the age of twenty-three I was married to Brooke Christine Mitchell. Four years later we tried to have our first child. We learned that neither of us could. Brooke cried for nearly two weeks.

But, as so often happens in life, from our hurts come our greatest blessings. Brooke and I made a decision that changed many lives: we adopted the first of our eight children, each of them taken from an environment of abuse or neglect. With each child we saved, a cycle has been broken. We now have more than a dozen grandchildren who know only security, peace, and a parent's love. What Grace planted in me will save generations from neglect and abuse. I do not take credit for this but I do take hope in it.

I believe there is a life after this one. I hope it is a place of second chances, a place where all things are made whole. That, to me, would be heaven. If there is such a place, I'd like to see Grace there. I'd like to see her without worry or pain. I'd like to sit with her and hear her sweet voice, feel her soft lips against mine and laugh until milk shoots from our noses. I hope to look with her into the flame of a candle and hear all about where she's been and where the world is going. Most of all, I hope to tell her how much I love her still. I don't deserve it, but I hope.

Maybe someday, through God's grace, I will.

A LETTER FROM
RICHARD PAUL EVANS

Dear Reader,

While the story you've just read is fiction, at this moment there are thousands of stories like Grace's happening in real life.

Through the blessing of your readership and the help of many friends, I have been able to establish The Christmas Box International, an organization dedicated to building emergency children's shelters and providing services for abused and neglected children. Since we started more than a decade ago, we have served more than twenty thousand children. Most of the children we help are young, sometimes just infants, and usually entering state custody or foster care for the first time.

With the release of this book we have launched an exciting new and massive project called **The Christmas Box Initiative**. Our goal is to help *every youth* in America who is aging out of foster care. Right now these youths face serious challenges including; crime, drug addiction, teen pregnancy, poverty, and suicide. With no one to help them, many of them return to abusive home situations or end up homeless and on the streets. We can make a difference. The Christmas Box Initiative is a four-phase plan:

Phase 1. Working with local child protective services, The Christmas Box International will provide Christmas Box Lifestart Kits to youths as they leave state care. These kits include simple but vital things youths need to start their transition to adulthood such as dinnerware, cooking utensils, a first aid kit, a tool kit, bed sheets, towels, and more, including important information to help these youths navigate life on their own. Giving these kits also connects us with these youths in a relationship of trust.

Phase 2. Assist communities in helping their own youth by creating local "Christmas Box Rooms." A Christmas Box Room would consist of a room or space supported by community members and agencies that would be used to collect and store items needed by youth in that area.

Phase 3. Assist in finding a mentor for each of these youths. A mentor could consist of an individual mentor or a mentoring family. This will be the most challenging of our goals but will eventually accomplish the most good.

Phase 4. Providing an information hotline and internet site to help these youth not only in crisis situations, but also in finding the many resources available to them, including housing and education.

Our ultimate goal is to help every one of these youths live happy, productive lives as law-abiding citizens and break the cycle of abuse and neglect they were raised with.

HOW CAN YOU HELP?

You can help by joining with Operation Kids in support of this program. Operation Kids is an international charity that has supported the Christmas Box House for nearly ten years. Their enthusiasm for this program includes a match of all donations received online. For only $100 you can provide a Christmas Box Lifestart Kit to a youth leaving foster care.

I know that you are probably already giving

to many important charities. But if just one out of twenty of my readers decides to help just one youth a year (about 27 cents a day) by donating to Operation Kids, your donation will result in the purchase of a Christmas Box Lifestart Kit for *every* transitioning foster child in America. Of course you or your business is welcome to assist as many youths as you like.

Will you be one of those special angels? I promise that one hundred percent of your donation will go to creating these kits, and Operation Kids supports that promise. Any overhead associated with this program is covered through my book sales and the support of many wonderful individuals and organizations like Operation Kids. To join our cause, go to www.operationkids.org/lifestart and click on LIFE-START KITS. Or call: 1-888-257-KIDS.

Thank you and God bless,
Richard Paul Evans

JOIN THE RICHARD PAUL EVANS MAILING LIST, GET A FREE GIFT *AND* HELP A CHILD

Join Richard's mailing list and you'll not only receive advance notice of Richard's book releases and events in your area but you'll also receive a free, downloadable audio copy of:

The First Gift of Christmas
Written and read by Richard Paul Evans

HELP A CHILD. Also, for everyone who joins Richard's mailing list, *Operation Kids* will donate $1 to The Christmas Box International to help abused and neglected youth.* To join now go to **RichardPaul-Evans.com** and click on the **Join Mailing List** button. Then type in your first name, state, and email address. (Note: Richard respects your privacy and does not share or sell his mailing list.)

If you are already on Richard's mailing list you may also receive these free gifts by following the directions on the **Join Mailing List** site.

* Offer good until December 31, 2009.

✦ ABOUT THE AUTHOR ✦

When Richard Paul Evans sat down to write *The Christmas Box*, he never imagined his book would become a number one bestseller. The quiet story of parental love and the true meaning of Christmas made history when it became simultaneously the number one hardcover and paperback book in the nation. Since then, he has written twelve consecutive *New York Times* best-sellers. He is one of the few authors in history to have hit both the fiction and nonfiction best-seller lists and has won several awards for his books, including the 1998 American Mothers Book

Award, two first-place Storytelling World Awards, and the 2005 Romantic Times Best Women's Novel of the Year Award.

Four of Evans's books have been made into major television productions, starring such acclaimed actors as Maureen O'Hara, James Earl Jones, Richard Thomas, Ellen Burstyn, Naomi Watts, Vanessa Redgrave, Christopher Lloyd, and Rob Lowe.

During the spring of 1997, Evans founded The Christmas Box House International, an organization devoted to building shelters and providing services for abused and neglected children. Such shelters are operational in Moab, Vernal, Ogden, and Salt Lake City, Utah. To date Christmas Box House facilities have served more than twenty thousand children. In addition, his book *The Sunflower* was the motivating factor in the creation of The Sunflower Orphanage in Peru. Evans was awarded the Volunteers of America National Empathy Award and the *Washington Times* Humanitarian of the Century Award. As an acclaimed speaker, Evans has shared the podium with such notable personalities as President George W. Bush, President George H. W. and Barbara Bush, former

British Prime Minister John Major, Ron Howard, Elizabeth Dole, Deepak Chopra, Steve Allen, and Bob Hope. Evans has been featured on the *Today* show, *The Glenn Beck Show,* CNN, CSPAN, and *Entertainment Tonight*, as well as in *Time, Newsweek, People, The New York Times, The Washington Post, Good Housekeeping, USA Today, TV Guide, Reader's Digest*, and *Family Circle*. Evans lives in Salt Lake City, Utah, with his wife, Keri, and their five children.